"Hugh Ashton does a fantastic job of continuing the Sherlock Holmes legacy in the true tradition and style of Sir Arthur Conan Doyle."

"The writing style completely recreates the work of Sir Arthur Conan Doyle and provides a perfect continuation of the famous adventures of the great detective. I plan to read all of these books, they are like finding treasure thought lost for many years."

"...the characters, from Holmes and Watson to Lestrade and all the minor characters appearing in the stories, are masterfully rendered in a way that is both faithful to the original and at the same time subtly innovative."

"Unlike Sir Arthur Conan Doyle, who got tired of his logical creation, Sherlock Holmes, Hugh Ashton clearly loves the character and his traits. I kept thinking that I was reading a more clever, sharper, wittier, just generally better writer, doing Conan Doyle like it should have been done."

"There is the feel of the stratified society, the scent of coal smoke in your nose, and the slightly foggy streets of 19th century London radiate around you as you read these stories... These are thoroughly enjoyable and completely authentic in feel and atmosphere, and we can almost hear Holmes whispering, ' Come, now; the game's afoot...and do bring your revolver with you.' "

THE DEATH

OF

CARDINAL TOSCA

The Death of Cardinal Tosca: An Untold Adventure of
Sherlock Holmes

Hugh Ashton

ISBN-10: 0615858643
ISBN-13: 978-0615858647

Published by Inknbeans Press, 2013

www.inknbeans.com

www.221BeanBakerStreet.info

Inknbeans Press,
25060 Hancock Avenue Bldg 103 Suite 458,
Murrieta CA 92562, USA

DEDICATION

 HIS book is dedicated to all those who love and treasure the life and work of the great detective, Mr. Sherlock Holmes of Baker-street.

PREFACE
BY HUGH ASHTON

Y researches into the life and work of the great detective Sherlock Holmes, and of his friend and biographer, Dr. John Watson, continue to produce excitement.

The dispatch-box deposited in the vaults of Cox & Co. has produced an unexpected gem from the depths—a case of Sherlock Holmes which was mentioned in *The Hound of the Baskervilles*, but has not yet seen the light of day. I provide a little more information about this in the Editor's Notes immediately before the story itself, which deals with several aspects of the British political scene of the day.

Be that as it may, there were several aspects of the original Sherlock Holmes canon which are still a puzzle to many readers. Doctor Watson was, I think we can all agree, a courageous and loyal friend of the great sleuth. But why, one may ask, would Sherlock Holmes, with his love of accuracy and precision, entrust the writing of his cases to a man who consistently made so many sloppy errors? Sherlockians delight in the puzzles and paradoxes to be found in the Canon, and come up with many ingenious ideas to explain them.

I have a very simple explanation, expounded at some length in an article which will appear in the Winter 2013 edition of *The Watsonian*, the journal of the John H. Watson Society.

Briefly stated, my thesis is that these " errors" and " contradictions" were introduced into the narrative by Sherlock Holmes himself. As a matter of sheer courtesy, if for no other reason, Watson would undoubtedly have shown to Holmes the drafts of the accounts of their adventures together before passing them on to Sir Arthur Conan Doyle, his literary agent.

Naturally, Holmes would want to keep some details of his methods a secret—after all, if criminals were made aware of these methods, they could avoid making mistakes in the future which would lead to their detection and arrest. For this reason, as well as the interests of State security, as exemplified in this account, we may take it as a given fact that Watson's accounts of his adventures with Sherlock Holmes are not to be taken as literal accounts of the facts as they occurred, any more than the dialogue he records is a literal transcription of the words spoken at those times.

Hugh Ashton
Kamakura, 2013
hashton@inknbeans.com

COLOPHON

E decided that this adventure of Sherlock Holmes deserved to be reproduced on paper in as authentic a fashion as was possible given modern desktop publishing and print-on-demand technology.

Accordingly, after consulting the reproductions of the original Holmes adventures as printed in *The Strand Magazine*, we decided to use the Monotype Bruce Old Style font from Bitstream as the body (10.5 on 13.2). Though it would probably look better letterpressed than printed using a lithographic or laser method, and is missing old-style numerals, it still manages to convey the feel of the original. The flowers are Bodoni Ornaments, which have a little more of a 19th-century appearance than some of the alternatives.

Chapter titles, page headers, and footers are in Baskerville (what else can one use for a Holmes story ?), and the decorative drop caps are in Romantique, which preserves the feel of the *Strand*'s original drop caps.

The punctuation is carried out according to the rules apparently followed by the *Strand*'s typesetters. These include double spacing after full stops (periods), spaces after opening quotation marks, and spaces on either side of punctuation such as question marks, exclamation marks and semi-colons. This seems to allow the type to breathe more easily, especially in long spoken and quoted exchanges, and we have therefore adopted this style here.

Some of the orthography has also been deliberately changed to match the original—for instance, " Baker Street" has become " Baker-street" throughout.

Acknowledgements

ANY THANKS TO ALL who have assisted in making this book. Writing may be a solitary craft, but the creation of a book is a team effort, including much hard work and support by people who never put pen to paper or finger to keyboard.

First, to my readers, who actually buy and read and enjoy my writing in sufficient quantities to continue to encourage me in my madness.

To Yoshiko, my wife, who remains baffled and amused by the growing list of books on our shelves with my name as author on the spine, and supports me in my quest to recreate the atmosphere of 221B Baker-street from a small Japanese town.

And to Jo, the Boss Bean at Inknbeans Press, who puts up with my unreasonable demands, and still manages to produce and promote my books.

CONTENTS

The Death of Cardinal Tosca

of

Cardinal Tosca

From the Dispatch-Box of
John H. Watson MD

An Untold Adventure of

Sherlock Holmes

As Discovered By
Hugh Ashton

EDITOR'S NOTE

*In the second box of Dr. Watson's papers (the " dispatch-box")
from London, I discovered a thick envelope, sealed with a wax seal
and the impression of a signet with the initial 'S'. On the back
flap were written, in that splendidly scrawling but legible hand
with which I am now familiar, the words " Not to be opened before
September 25, 2014".*

*Dare one disobey the instructions of Sherlock Holmes ? Dare
one cross swords with the great detective and defy his will, even
long after his death ?*

*For a long time this envelope stood on my desk, Holmes' words
ringing in my ears as I contemplated them. In my mind's eye I
could see all those famous actors who have sought to bring back to
life that most famous adventurer of the London fogs. Basil Rath-
bone's finger wagged at me. Benedict Cumberbatch's sneer of disdain was directed at me. And Jeremy Brett simply turned his*

back on me in disgust.

But yet... I had to know more. What was there in this envelope that had to remain hidden for so long? It was almost certainly another adventure that Holmes and Watson had shared, which had not been published, for reasons unknown. But what? The game was afoot.

With a prayer to the saint who protects the overly curious, I slit open the envelope. As well as the expected manuscript, written in Watson's crabbed hand, some newspaper clippings dealing with the outbreak of the Great War, and a letter, written in another, strangely familiar style, appeared. It took me a little time, but I recognised the handwriting as that of Sir Arthur Conan Doyle, John Watson's literary agent. On reading this, I realised that I had stumbled upon a matter—the death of Cardinal Tosca—which was of great significance at the time it was written, and still had resonance today.

Naturally, I could not resist reading Watson's account, and to my surprise, found that the case of Cardinal Tosca was much more complex and had far more wide-reaching implications than I would ever have imagined.

Watson writes about his friend's "famous investigation of the sudden death of Cardinal Tosca—an inquiry which was carried out by him at the express desire of His Holiness the Pope" in Black Peter, but never tells us more. Many people have guessed that Holmes was summoned to Rome to investigate a death in the Vatican. The truth is actually more complex than that and involves Mycroft once again—who seems to have acted as the éminence grise of the late Victorian and early Edwardian governments.

I reflected on whether to publish this case, and decided that the dangers to the British way of life that Holmes (and Doyle) feared in 1914 no longer applied. The roles of religion and the monarchy in the life of the nation have changed almost beyond recognition, and the problems that beset the Edwardians have largely been

*resolved—at least to the point where they would no longer be an is-
sue in determining the publicity or otherwise of this case.*

PART I – THE CARDINAL'S DEATH

Monsignor Mahoney

–

The Diogenes Club, London

O F all the cases in which Sherlock Holmes was involved, one of the more interesting was the case which concerned the death of Cardinal Tosca. As my readers will remember reading in the newspapers of the day, His Eminence was visiting England when he succumbed to a stroke while staying at his London hotel, much to the regret of the Catholic Church in this country, on behalf of which he had been a loyal advocate in the Curia. His passing was also publicly mourned by the Archbishop of Canterbury, who declared that the Cardinal had done more than anyone to bring about a true reconciliation between the Church of England, and that of Rome. It was discreetly given out that, given the delicate state of the European diplomatic situation at the time, Sherlock Holmes had been asked to pronounce definitively that there had been no foul play. This announcement attracted considerable notice, and questions were asked as to the wisdom of employing a private investigator in the case, rather than the official police force.

In the event, though, public honour was satisfied by the public statement of Inspector Stanley Hopkins of the Metropolitan Police Force, who informed the public that, in his opinion, Holmes' findings were in complete accordance with the facts as he understood them.

The truth, however, was a very different matter, and one in which Sherlock Holmes and I found ourselves deeply involved in a business of whose real nature few were aware. The unvarnished truth of this incident was considered to be too explosive to be made public, but I consider that after all this time, they may be safely revealed. Indeed, there is much to be said for the case that they should be revealed at this time of national peril.*

---

*   Editor's note: It is unclear to what " national peril" Watson is referring here. However, since the papers describing this case were found between newspaper cuttings of the early autumn of 1914, it is likely that Watson was referring to the outbreak of the First World War, in the run-up to which Holmes and Watson played their parts, as described in His Last Bow. Possibly this final adventure brought back to Watson his memories of this earlier case, which was likewise of national significance. However, it should be noted that attached to the back of this manuscript was a note from Sir Arthur Conan Doyle, regretting that he was unable to act as Watson's literary agent in this instance (attached as an appendix).

As with so many cases of this nature, the initial summons came through Sherlock Holmes' older brother, Mycroft. I was building up my medical practice at the time, and was living away from Baker-street, though visiting my friend as often as my work would permit, when we would often spend an evening dining, and afterwards smoking our pipes and engaging in companionable conversation, during the course of which Holmes would frequently inform me of the details of some of his recent cases.

It was on one such evening that I mounted the steps to the well-known rooms at 221B Baker-street, and was about to knock on the door, when it suddenly opened, to reveal Holmes, dressed in his overcoat.

" Just the man whom I need to see at this moment," he smiled with pleasure. " I am just on my way out, and would be grateful if you would accompany me. Had you not turned up when you did, I would have given Mrs. Hudson instructions to admit you and to request you to wait for my return. As it is..."

" Where are we going ? " I asked as I followed him down the stairs.

" To the Diogenes Club," he answered briefly.

" Brother Mycroft ? "

He nodded. " I received a telegram from him not fifteen minutes ago. Here, see for yourself." He reached in his pocket and pulled out a folded paper.

I read out loud, " ' MEET ME AT CLUB IMMEDIATELY ON CONFIDENTIAL MATTER RE TOSCA. MYCROFT.'. It certainly seems as though there is something of importance. But 'Tosca' ? Does this refer to the opera ? "

Holmes laughed. " I am certain that it does not. Mycroft has little interest in artistic matters. It is almost certainly concerned with the visit to this country by His

Eminence Cardinal Pietro Tosca, the emissary from the Vatican."

" I remember seeing his name in the newspapers, but I took little notice of it, I confess."

" He is here to negotiate some business on behalf of His Holiness, I believe. No doubt Mycroft will tell us more when we meet him." As we spoke, Holmes hailed a cab. The journey passed in relative silence, my friend seemingly preferring to sit in silence rather than make conversation, and I was sufficiently acquainted with his moods not to intrude.

On our arrival at the Club, Holmes gave his name to the porter, and we were shown without delay to the Strangers' Room of that remarkable institution, where conversation between members is not only discouraged, but forbidden, save for the chamber to which we were conducted.

Our eyes beheld the massive form of Mycroft Holmes as we entered, but it was the other occupant of the room who excited my curiosity. Though clad in the usual attire of a man about town, his garments somehow appeared to be of a foreign cut, and to hang strangely on his small frame. His lined face was deeply tanned, but with striking blue eyes, and his hair, cut shorter than was fashionable at the time, had originally been dark, but now had almost entirely turned to silver. Both men rose to their feet to greet us.

" Who is this, Mr. Holmes ? " demanded the stranger of Mycroft Holmes, in a strange accent that I had difficulty placing, though it had more than a touch of Irish to it, as he indicated me, and settled himself in his seat once more.

Sherlock's brother waved his flipper-like hand negligently. " You need not trouble yourself, sir," was his rejoinder. " This is Dr. Watson, who is my brother's faithful companion and biographer. Anything you may have heard about brother Sherlock other than what I have told you is through the good graces of Watson here, who has recounted his exploits in a most entertaining manner."

" Hardly scientific, according to him, though," I laughed.

" Be that as it may. I would like to introduce you, Sherlock, and Dr. Watson, to—"

" Monsignor— ? " interrupted Sherlock.

" Indeed, Monsignor Mahoney, secretary to the late Cardinal Tosca," said Mycroft.

Both Holmes and the prelate started to speak at the same time, stopped, and started again simultaneously.

" No, after you, Monsignor," Sherlock Holmes eventually said, following several halts and starts.

" How in the world did you know of my profession and rank when you addressed me just now ? " asked Mahoney, obviously bewildered.

Holmes smiled. " The way in which you sat in that chair just now showed me that you are unaccustomed to wearing trousers. When my brother informed me in his telegram that this business concerned Cardinal Tosca, I could easily make the inference that a cassock is more your everyday attire than a suit of clothes. And the purple socks, of course, inform me of your rank." Mycroft Holmes said nothing, but I noticed his slightly sardonic smile as his younger brother related his findings.

Mahoney smiled. " It seems I must work harder at preserving my incognito."

" But Mycroft," said Sherlock Holmes. " You referred just now to the late Cardinal Tosca, did you not ? How can that be ? "

Mycroft's expression was serious. " Cardinal Tosca died two days ago. The matter has not been publicly announced, and the general public is still under the impression that he is suffering from a slight cold, which has prevented him from making public appearances at present."

Holmes' face grew grave. " I take it this is no ordinary death, then ? " he asked.

" By no means," Mycroft answered. " It is murder."

" Murder ? " I exclaimed. " But who could have done such a thing ? Why would anyone wish to do so ? "

" This is precisely why I have invited my brother to investigate the case," said Mycroft Holmes, with a touch of asperity.

" I am somewhat engaged," protested Holmes. " The doings at Atherstoke Grange—"

" It is the brother-in-law, who is in debt as a result of his improvidence at the races," interrupted Mycroft abruptly. " Did you learn nothing from your examination of the driveway ? "

Sherlock Holmes looked somewhat abashed. " I had not considered the evidence in that light," he said. " However, I will reexamine the facts taking that opinion into account."

" Hardly an opinion, dear boy. It is the only conclusion that a rational mind can reach. But you will have the kindness to resume your study of these trivia after you have investigated the problem before us here and now."

" Very well, then. Perhaps I had better hear the facts."

" And so you shall," replied Mycroft. " Monsignor Mahoney is the man to provide them." He gestured to the prelate, who sat forward in his chair, and addressed us.

" Let me begin," he started his speech, " by telling you something of myself and of my relations with Cardinal Tosca. I have been in the service of the Church for over thirty-five years. I have been addressed by my current title since my appointment as a pronotary apostolic some five years ago, and I became the personal confidential secretary of His Eminence some three years ago. He was not an easy man for whom to work. It is said '*de mortuis nil nisi bonum*', Mr. Holmes, but in truth, I cannot say that it was a pleasure to serve under him.

" My nature is perhaps too easy-going—indeed, it is a fault to which I regularly confess—but Cardinal Tosca is— or rather was, I should say—very strict in his demands for the work carried out on his behalf. For example, he would tolerate no corrections of any kind on a letter which carried his name. Should I make a single mistake in copying or writing such an epistle, I would invariably be required to write the whole page again. When we were travelling together, everything had to be exactly to his wishes. When he bathed, the water had to be at the precise temperature to which he was accustomed, and so on.

" He could display a kind and generous side on occasion, though. For example, I suffered from influenza last winter, and he nursed me with his own hands, and ensured that I had proper care for the whole period of my indisposition. Let no-one say of him that he lacked Christian charity towards his fellow-men. But at the same time, he was not an easy master to serve. I disliked working with him, but in the service of the Church, we must all take the tasks to which we are assigned, and it is not our place to attempt to change our lot."

Here, the cleric stopped, and looked at Mycroft, seemingly unsure as to how he should continue. On receiving an almost imperceptible nod, he resumed his narrative.

" I tell you these things in all honesty. It would be foolish of me to conceal them from you, and you would no doubt discover them for yourselves as you investigate. Now, I should tell you of the reasons for the visit to this country by His Eminence and me.

" You may well be aware that the Holy Father himself is personally deeply saddened by the schism between the Church of Rome, and the Church here in England. It would be one of his deepest joys should England return to the fold. You may imagine the joy in the Curia when we heard that a prominent member of the British Royal family had expressed interest in receiving instruction in order to be received into the Church.

" Appropriate measures were taken, and instruction was provided, albeit secretly, given the extraordinary delicacy of the situation."

" The monarch is, after all, the head of the Church of England," Holmes commented. " Any public move towards Rome by a member of the monarch's family could be seen as an act of disloyalty to the country as a whole."

" Indeed it could," agreed the priest. " Though such an act would be a matter for the individual's private conscience, His Holiness was well aware that there would be strong popular feeling in England against such a move, were it to be made public without due preparation.

" It was known that Mr. Mycroft Holmes here would be able to prepare the smoothest path for such an event to take place—"

" I have helped the Holy See with a few small matters in the past," said Mycroft. " My name is known in the Vatican as one who is prepared to listen."

" Not only as one who is prepared to listen, Mr. Holmes," corrected Mahoney, " but as one who is prepared to take appropriate action as required. Your name is regarded most highly within the Curia, you may believe me.

" In any event, His Eminence was ordered by His

Holiness to come to Britain to survey the land, as it were. Not only did he speak fluent English, but he had a gift for pouring diplomatic oil on troubled waters, which was somewhat at variance, I admit, with the distinctly un-diplomatic fashion with which he could treat those under him. Naturally I was to accompany him on this mission.

" It was arranged that he would make his visit under the cover of an official visitation to the Archdiocese of West-minster. In truth, this visit was to be carried out by His Eminence, but the true reason for the visit would be the meeting with the Royal personage."

" Where were you lodged ? In an hotel ? " asked Holmes.

" No, it was decided that we should be staying at Lord Ledbury's country seat in Hertfordshire. His Lordship is the head of one of the oldest Catholic families in England, as I am sure you are aware. Given that we were supposed-ly inspecting the state of the archdiocese, it was felt that this would provide a suitable distance from the church it-self. In addition, the Royal personage visiting Lord Led-bury would excite significantly less comment than if they were to visit the Archbishop. The discretion afforded by a private residence of this type was seen as a distinct advantage."

" I understand," Holmes added drily.

" Lord Ledbury was a most gracious host, and provid-ed His Eminence and myself with splendid accommoda-tion. Not only did our rooms provide the highest possible degree of comfort, but we were also supplied with every fa-cility to carry out our business."

" Of what, precisely, did this business consist ? " asked Holmes.

" We met various members of the Cabinet with regard to

the proposed meeting of His Eminence with the Royal personage. These meetings were generally held at night—"

"—thereby confirming the opinion of many Englishmen regarding the way in which the Roman Church operates—that is, by way of secrecy and subterfuge," broke in Holmes.

The priest flushed, but it was Mycroft Holmes who answered his brother. " I advised against such night meetings from the first, Sherlock, for precisely the reason that you have given. However, I was overruled at the highest level." He sighed. " A case of pearls before swine, if I may use a Biblical phrase in this context, Monsignor."

" Oh, quite, quite," cried the cleric. " By day we were engaged in our ostensible purpose, that is to say, the visitation to the archdiocese. The evenings were given over to the other meetings."

" What was discussed in those meetings ? " asked Holmes.

" I fear I am not at liberty to tell you that," the other answered, primly.

" Then, Mycroft," said Holmes, rising to his feet, " I fear you have wasted both your time and my own by asking me to come here. There is little point in asking me to assist you in your business if I am not even to be told the nature of the game that is being played out."

" Calm yourself, Sherlock, and hear the story out to its conclusion. Then you may decide for yourself if the business is indeed relevant to your part in it."

" Very well." Sherlock Holmes took his seat with what appeared to me to be a poor grace. " Pray continue, Monsignor."

" As I say, every facility was provided by Lord Ledbury during these meetings. I suppose I may tell you that these meetings were, to my mind, successful, even if I do not tell you of their exact purpose."

" You say that they were successful to your mind ? How did the Cardinal regard them ? "

" He never spoke of his feelings openly, but to me, who had worked with him in the past, it was obvious that he was satisfied with our progress."

" You mentioned meetings with members of the British Cabinet." Holmes persisted in his questioning. " Am I permitted to enquire as to the outcome of the meeting with the member of the Royal family ? "

" You may certainly enquire, but I cannot tell you, for the simple reason that the meeting never took place. It was planned for late yesterday evening."

" By which time, Cardinal Tosca was already dead, as I understand it."

" That is correct. Maybe I should acquaint you with some of the particulars surrounding that event ? "

" I would appreciate your doing so." Holmes' tone was cold.

" Very well. Today is Wednesday, is it not ? On Monday night, then, no meetings were planned. His Eminence proposed to me that we review the papers and the records of the meetings that had been held so far so that we might be ready for the visit on the following night. Accordingly, I got out the papers that were needed for this review, but before we started, at eight o'clock we ate dinner."

" With Lord Ledbury and his family ? " asked Holmes.

" No, we ate alone in the small family dining-room, which had been reserved for us during the period of our stay. Lord Ledbury and his family, we were given to understand by the butler who served us with our meal, were absent from the house that evening, attending some social function."

" On the other days of your visit, had you been taking your meals with your host ? "

" As it happened, this only occurred once. His Eminence was by nature an abstemious man. His diet often consisted of little more than bread and water, and he felt it would appear as an insult to his host were he to appear at table but not to partake of the food offered to him."

" Did he attempt to inflict the same regimen on you ? " asked Holmes.

" He gave me to understand that it would be preferable to him were I to follow his example. However, the spirit is willing, but the flesh..." Here, the cleric rubbed an ample belly and smiled ruefully. " However, he had sufficient humanity to recognise that his way of life was not for all to follow. In any event, referring back to Monday night, once the meal had been completed, he proposed that we remain at the dining-table, which would serve us for the examination and study of papers on which we were currently at work."

Holmes sighed. " I take it that I am not to be informed as to the contents of these papers ? "

" I am sorry, but these are also a matter of some secrecy. They are connected with the subject of our visit, naturally, but their exact contents must, for the moment at least, remain hidden.

" The butler cleared the table, and we told him of our intention to remain in the room, to which he informed us that if we preferred, he would bring our coffee to us in the dining-room, rather than the sitting-room that had been reserved for our use. Though, as I say, His Eminence was abstemious, if not actually ascetic, in his habits, if he had a leaning towards the vice of gluttony, it was in the matter of coffee, and he gladly agreed to this.

" The coffee was duly brought in—"

" By whom ? " interjected Holmes.

" Once again this was the butler, Alvarez. He was the only servant whom we saw that evening and indeed most evenings. Lord Ledbury had apparently placed us under Alvarez's particular care, and we had little contact with other members of the household. Before the coffee had been poured, His Eminence asked me—or rather, given his nature, it was more in the form of an order—to go upstairs and fetch the papers which we were proposing to examine.

" When I returned, I discovered that he had already consumed one cup of coffee, and was complaining of stomach pains. This was not unusual for him."

" When you say that this was not unusual, are you referring to the pains or to the complaints regarding them ? "

The priest looked at Sherlock Holmes with something approaching respect. " That, sir, is a very subtle question, is it not ? I was able to discern that he was in some discomfort relatively frequently following his post-prandial coffee. He was not of a type that complained of his ills, though. Such a complaint was indeed unusual for him."

" How did he take his coffee on that evening ? "

" The same way in which he usually took it, that is to say, without milk or sugar."

I broke in. " If his usual fare was as simple as you have described, little more than bread and water, I would expect some sort of abdominal pain to follow the ingestion of hot black coffee."

Mahoney smiled ruefully. " Do you think that I had not informed him of that myself ? It was not my place to tell him what he should and should not eat, but it appeared to me that his habits were not of benefit to his health, and I had taken it upon myself on several occasions in the past to let him know that I considered them to be unwise. However, my words had little or no effect on him. He was a stubborn man, and was unwilling to take advice, however well-meaning, from others.

" In any event, he and I went through the papers, only to discover that one of the most important of them had been left upstairs. I mentioned before that he was a strict taskmaster, and this occasion proved to be no exception. His words to me regarding my omission were biting and sarcastic—out of respect for the dead, I will not repeat them here, but they cut me to the quick. They were especially wounding to me, since the butler had entered the room during part of his tirade—there is no other word to describe his flow of words, sir.

" Being more than a little embarrassed at being put on the spot in this way in front of the servants, I was happy to leave the room in search of the papers." Here, the priest felt in his sleeve, and brought out a handkerchief, which he used to mop his brow. " Now comes the terrible part of my tale. I went upstairs to look for the paper, which I could not believe I had left out of the packet that I had brought downstairs for examination. From the stairs, I noticed Alvarez leave his butler's pantry and make his way towards the kitchen. I believe he also saw me, and will be happy to confirm that point, should you ever have occasion to ask him. When I reached the room from which I had taken the papers, I searched for the missing document high and low, on the desk, and throughout the room, but was unable to discover it. I was fearful of His Eminence's wrath if I returned downstairs without it, and I continued searching, but it failed to come to light. I therefore determined that I must, after all, have brought the paper downstairs with the others, and it had somehow become folded in or otherwise confused with the papers we had been examining, and it had been overlooked. I therefore made my way downstairs to the dining-room, and there I beheld His Eminence, quite dead."

" How could you be sure he was dead ? " asked Holmes.

" I have never seen the face of a living man in such a rigid expression of terror," the other told us. " And I may tell you that as a priest I have seen my share of the dead, both those who have died peacefully, and those who have died through acts of violence. I served in the British Army many years ago," he offered in answer to Holmes' raised eyebrows.

" How had he died ? "

" It was not obvious to me at first, but when I approached closer, I could see the hilt of a knife protruding from his chest."

" A knife ? One of the dinner knives ? " asked Holmes.

" No, it was a paperknife in the shape of a Toledo blade. It was the property of His Eminence, and it always accompanied him in his travels. If he had been of another type of mind, I would have said that it was a charm of some kind, but he was far from subscribing to that sort of superstition. I believe it had some sort of sentimental association for him, if that word may be used in connection with him, since he had served the archdiocese of Toledo in the past as its archbishop."

" Did he typically carry this knife on his person ? "

" No, that is the extraordinary thing, Mr. Holmes. I could have sworn that I saw the knife upstairs when I fetched the papers the first time, and naturally I left it there, having no use for it. Somehow the knife must have found its way downstairs by means of another hand. The same hand that planted it in the body of His Eminence, I have no doubt."

" No doubt," repeated Holmes. " And the paper that was missing ? The one for which you had been dispatched upstairs ? "

Mahoney shrugged his shoulders. " It is still missing."

" What did you do ? "

" I confess, Mr. Holmes, that I was terrified. It was inconceivable to me that Cardinal Tosca could have been killed in such a mysterious way. I prayed for the dead man's soul, and when I heard Alvarez approaching the door to enter to remove the coffee service, I shouted through the closed door that he was not to enter, but he was to send a telegram to Mr. Mycroft Holmes informing him that the Cardinal had suffered a seizure, and when Lord Ledbury returned, he was to ask his lordship to vis-it me in the dining-room." He broke off and passed a hand over his face. " Maybe it is not my place, but it seems to me that I may be able to shed a little light on the mystery." Holmes said nothing, but inclined his head slightly to in-dicate that the other should continue his narrative. " The butler, Alvarez. There is something that strikes me as be-ing false about him and I am suspicious of his motives."

" He is from which country ? His name would suggest a Hispanic or Latin American origin."

" From Spain, I believe. I have heard it said that he was from Toledo. There may be some sort of Latin grudge or revenge at work from His Eminence's previous appoint-ment in that town."

" That is entirely possible, of course. Let us return to the sequence of events. You dispatched a telegram to my brother. To where was this sent ? "

" The telegram was sent to my office in Whitehall, and

then delivered by messenger to me at the club here," explained Mycroft, " but it was impossible for me to make the journey at that time of night. However, I happen to know that Lord Ledbury had a telephone installed in the Hall—indeed, this circumstance formed one of the reasons why I selected him and Ledbury Hall as a host for the Cardinal—and I was able to make use of the club telephone here to speak with Monsignor Mahoney."

" You have a telephone here in the Diogenes Club ? " enquired Holmes of Mycroft, with a smile. " Does not this somewhat go against the spirit of the foundation ? "

" It does," admitted his brother, " but I have found it to be an advantage in my work. I am able to receive information and to issue orders without troubling myself to stir out of this building. I therefore commanded the installation of the instrument in a sound-proofed lobby to proceed some months ago.

" As I was saying," he continued, " I instructed Monsignor Mahoney here that he should admit no one to the room except Lord Ledbury on his return, and to give out to the servants that His Eminence had somewhat recovered and was in no need of further assistance. The situation was indeed grave, and the next morning I rose early and made my way to the scene at Ledbury Hall."

" I am quite frankly amazed at your action," commented Sherlock Holmes. As he had remarked to me on another occasion, his brother's movements were as set and as regular as those of a tram, and for Mycroft Holmes to depart from his habits in this way was a *rara avis* indeed.

" I could do no less," his brother answered. " A constitutional crisis was afoot, not so much by reason of the death of the Cardinal, as of the fact that the paper to which Mahoney here has just alluded is missing."

" Very well. May I ask you," addressing himself to Mahoney, " what was the reaction of Lord Ledbury when he returned ? "

" Naturally, he was horrified by what had occurred. I chose not to inform him of the missing paper, as that was of no direct concern to him. I stayed in that dreadful room, Mr Holmes, all night, with the dead body of the Cardinal. I prayed for his soul, and I prayed that those who were responsible for his death would be brought to justice."

" Mahoney here was in the room when I arrived at Ledbury Hall," confirmed Mycroft Holmes. " With his help, I made a search for the missing paper, but was able to establish for myself that it was indeed missing."

" Since we are discussing this privately," said Sherlock Holmes, " I must assume that the official police have not been called in on this case."

" Nor will they be, until you have investigated the matter, Sherlock and come to some conclusions. This is one of those situations where the fewer who know of the details, the better."

" I take it that you will wish me to make my way to Ledbury Hall, and view the scene of the crime ? "

" Naturally."

" And will I be permitted to view the body ? "

" The Cardinal's body is still in the place where it was discovered. Everything is as it was when Mahoney discovered it."

Sherlock Holmes looked at his brother in amazement. " Do you mean to tell me, Mycroft, that you have allowed a dead body to remain in that room for now," he pulled out his watch and examined it, " somewhat in excess of thirty-six hours ? "

Mycroft Holmes inclined his great head. " That is correct," he confirmed.

" Then why in the name of all that is holy did you not contact me yesterday ? "

" I was awaiting instructions from Rome," replied his brother. " After searching for the missing paper, my first action was to send a telegram to the Vatican, explaining the situation, and requesting some guidance on the course of action that they felt would be most beneficial to all parties concerned. The answer came within two hours, and bore the name of His Holiness himself, requesting that you would be assigned to the case. Your reputation, thanks to Watson here, has obviously extended to the Holy See."

Holmes shrugged. " I understand," he said. " Very well, it seems that I have little choice in this matter. Let us start immediately."

" Before you start, Sherlock, there are one or two things that I wish to discuss with you in private. I mean no offence to you, Monsignor, but I would prefer it if you were to wait outside while I inform my brother of these matters. Please make your way to Ledbury Hall and inform his Lordship of my brother's imminent arrival."

" I will do that, and rest assured that there is no offence taken, believe me. I recognise that you, like myself, have secrets that are not for all ears," replied the cleric as he rose to his feet. He said these words with an expression that appeared almost to be gloating, and opened the door to leave the room. I likewise rose to depart, but Mycroft Holmes waved me back to my seat.

" You may stay, Doctor," he told me. When the door had closed behind Mahoney, and Sherlock Holmes had discreetly verified that the priest was at a safe distance, by opening the door and peering out before closing it again,

Mycroft Holmes rested his head in his hands and slowly looked up at his brother. For the first time I noticed the fatigue in his face. " Sherlock, I did not want to provide all the details in front of that Roman Irishman, but a grave constitutional crisis hangs on this case."

" So you said before. What is its nature ? "

" It concerns the Royal personage who was mentioned earlier. I have certain knowledge that this person has already converted to Roman Catholicism. This is an indisputable fact, and it is causing great concern in the present Government, I can tell you. Mahoney was being disingenuous at best when he told you of the purpose of Tosca's visit to this country. The Cardinal's mission to England was to seek to persuade the Royal personage to make a public declaration of his beliefs. You need not ask how I discovered this, but I was aware that this was Tosca's aim before he even set out from Rome. I was deputed by the Prime Minister to manage the affair, and you may imagine that I was not anxious that Tosca should succeed. Abhorrent as it may appear to you, I confess to feeling some relief regarding the death of the Cardinal at this point."

" I take it that this is the Royal individual concerned ? " said his brother, scribbling a name on a piece of paper torn from his notebook, and passing it to Mycroft, who glanced at it and nodded before passing it to me. I read the name with a sense of astonishment, and passed the paper back to my friend, who flicked it into the fire, where it was instantly consumed by the flames.

" This person has converted, as I say, and in the event of his succeeding to the Throne, I have it on the best of authorities that he would seek to abolish the Church of England, and place it under Rome once more, as it was in the days before Henry VIII. He would surrender his place as head of the Church of England, and that institution, as we know and understand it, would cease to exist. It is quite conceivable that the effect would also affect the Empire. There might be some rejoicing among the Irish element in Australia, but other than that..."

" This is a monstrous business ! " I exclaimed. " If what you describe were to come to pass, there would be civil war or some such thing throughout the land."

" It is not likely that he will succeed, though," remarked Sherlock Holmes. " It seems a most improbable eventuality."

" There is more chance of its occurring than you might imagine," his brother said, shaking his head sadly. " The Heir is not in good health, it is reported, and is in any case not as young as he was. There is also the possibility that some anarchist or other madman might make an attempt on his life which would place him of whom we speak in direct succession."

We considered this in silence for some moments. " You make the situation sound grave," I said to Mycroft.

" It is grave."

" Surely he can be prevented from making such a move ? " asked Sherlock Holmes. " Even if he is one of the Royal family, he could be prevented from making an announcement, especially since the Cardinal is no longer around to persuade him."

" There is worse. The paper that was described as missing is a letter from His Grace to His Holiness, written some months back, and promising faithfully that in the event of his taking the Throne, the Church of England will cease to be. Even if he were never to succeed, the public knowledge of this letter would be a catastrophe."

" Pooh. Denounce it as a forgery."

" It would seem easy to make such a move, but consider it as I have done. By doing as you suggest, we would impugn the credibility of the Roman church—a move which would hardly endear us to the indigenous Irish population, who are fractious enough as it is. And the word of a politician against one of the Royal family ? Even if the statesman were to be believed by the majority, there would still be many who would remain sceptical. No, Sherlock, the discovery and publication of this letter are risks that the nation can ill afford. I fear that Mahoney's motives in this matter are the same as those of his late master, whatever personal differences he may have had with him, and he would seek any opportunity to weaken the British government. You must ensure that the letter does not fall into his hands, Sherlock, or if it has, you must find a way to relieve him of it."*

" Recovery of the letter is more important than discovery

---

*   Editor's note: Watson is careful not to name this Royal personage, but it can be none other than George, Duke of York, the eldest surviving son of the Prince of Wales (Edward VII), who eventually succeeded his father as George V. His elder brother, Albert Victor, had died some years earlier. There is some support for this deduction, as is shown by his rejection of the older form of the Accession Declaration to be made at his coronation, a part of which read in the original form, " there is not any Transubstantiation of the elements of bread and wine into the Body and Blood of Christ at or after the consecration thereof by any person whatsoever: and that the invocation or adoration of the Virgin Mary or any other Saint, and the Sacrifice of the Mass, as they are now used in the Church of Rome, are superstitious and idolatrous".

of the identity of the killer ? "

" One may well lead you to the other."

" Indeed so. And Watson here is permitted to accompany me to Ledbury Hall ? "

" I would expect nothing less," said his brother. " Doctor Watson has proved his patriotism and his discretion in so many cases, that I trust him as I trust you in these matters. The opinion of a medical man of such ability regarding the cause of death may also prove to be of interest—indeed of value."

I was gratified by these words, for I knew Mycroft Holmes to be a reticent, almost cold, man who was not in the habit of bestowing compliments lightly.

" Excellent. We will be off, then, to Ledbury. Allow me time to collect some of my apparatus" (by which Holmes referred to his lenses and the small tool-kit that he carried on such occasions) " from Baker-street, and we will make our way to Hertfordshire."

" Do so with all speed. Report back to me by telegram on any points of interest. The usual cypher. Remember that the fate of this nation may rest in your hands."

Lord Ledbury

–

Ledbury Hall

"RE you acquainted with Lord Ledbury ? " Holmes asked me as we took
our seats in the train to Hertfordshire.

    " I have not yet had the pleasure," I
told him.

    " Oh, it was no great pleasure when I last encountered
him, I assure you. At that time he was a junior Cabinet
Minister, but since he left the Government some years ago,
he may be a little less acerbic in his manner, and be slightly more welcoming. Admittedly, the circumstances of our
last meeting were somewhat less than favourable. He was
one of those peripherally involved in the business with

Eduardo Lucas.* I fear that on that occasion, he felt that I was overstepping the bounds of my authority, despite the fact that the Prime Minister himself had commissioned me to look into the matter. I am unsure as to how he will regard my appointment in this case."

" At any event, Holmes, I trust that you will use all the diplomatic skill of which I know you to be capable. If what your brother has told you is true, this business could provoke chaos and anarchy in our streets."

Holmes smiled his thin smile. " Very well, I will endeavour to behave myself as you request." He leaned back and drew meditatively on his pipe. " What did you make of our Monsignor, by the by ? "

" His story seemed thin to me at times."

" To me, also. But he did not strike me as an unintelligent man. What did you make of his remarks concerning the Spanish butler ? "

" I would expect a priest, with his understanding of human nature, which you must assume a priest would acquire in the course of his duties, to be a fair judge of character. Quite possibly there is some truth in the matter."

" That is true, I suppose. If he were to invent a story, I would expect it to be one with more subtlety and perhaps a touch more plausibility. That leads me to believe for now that unlikely and improbable as his story may be, it may nonetheless be substantially the truth. But there is another matter that gives me concern, and that is the phrase that Monsignor Mahoney used when he left us. Do you recall it ? "

" It was something regarding secrets, if I remember

---

*   Editor's note: as recounted in *The Second Stain*

correctly."

" Indeed. He told us that he had his secrets. Now what in the world could he signify by that ? "

" I took it to mean little more than what he had learned in the confessional. Romish priests seem absurdly proud of that particular aspect of their calling."

" More than some doctors ? " Holmes laughed.

" Touché," I admitted. " But you must confess that it seems a likely explanation."

" Indeed I do, and you may well be correct. He could, of course, be referring to the missing letter, possibly unaware of the fact that brother Mycroft was fully cognisant of its contents. However, I am more inclined to your theory. Is it not common practice for a senior prelate to confess to a more junior, his personal chaplain ? "

" I believe that is the case, yes."

" And often the chaplain will also serve as the prelate's secretary ? "

" I begin to catch your drift. If Mahoney was in possession of some secret which was previously known only to the late Cardinal, and which had been revealed to him in confession, then that would account for his manner, would it not ? "

" Aye, that it would. But the nature of such a secret eludes me for the present. We must keep our ears open, and listen for anything that may lead us to discover it. I fear such clues will be few and far between, however." He flung himself back in his seat, and seemed to become lost in thought. A notion appeared to cross his brow, and he addressed himself to me once more. " Do you believe that my brother's gloomy prognostications are somewhat over-done ? " he asked me. " Do you really credit the notion that this nation could come to blows with itself over a matter of religion such as this ? "

" I do," I answered him. " There are many in this country who take their belief in these things much more seriously than do you. There are still those who will happily burn the Pope in effigy on November 5, and consider themselves as good patriotic Englishmen for doing so. It is sad, I agree, that there is so much hatred and intolerance in this country of ours, but it is a fact." I considered the matter a little more. " And there is another side to the coin. There is, as you know, a considerable number of Irishmen who wish home rule, or even complete political independence from England, for their country. The vast majority of these are of the Catholic faith, and were it to be made public that His Grace shared their belief, there is no knowing what might be the result of this."

" You are my touchstone in these things, Watson," he told me. " I live a life so divorced from such matters that I could not begin to pronounce on them with any pretence to authority, and it gave me a start when my brother professed himself to be so convinced of the ruin that would ensue. But when you and Mycroft agree, then I am tempted to assume the worst."

" You talk of assuming the worst. Let us assume for now that this particular outcome will not occur. One event that I am personally dreading, however, is the thought of examining a body that has remained untouched in a house for nearly two days. It is far from being an attractive proposition. It is true that I have encountered worse on the battlefield, but I had rashly assumed that those days were behind me."

" I confess that I cannot condone Mycroft's decision to leave the scene of the murder in its original state. It is true, of course, that any disturbance in such circumstances is to be deplored from the point of view of the scientific investigator, but even so..."

" I am surprised that Mahoney permitted it," I ventured.

Sherlock Holmes smiled. " Mycroft can be extraordinarily persuasive at times. I have many memories from my youth of those powers of his. I do not think that Mahoney may have had much freedom in the matter."

" In any event, it is not an event that I anticipate with any degree of pleasure." As I spoke, the train started to slow as we arrived at the station closest to Ledbury Hall, and Holmes and I alighted. We were greeted at the station by a trap, driven by a man who introduced himself as one of Lord Ledbury's grooms.

" His Lordship sent me down to meet you gentleman. The priest has gone before. He arrived on the previous train, and told us you were coming. You're a doctor, sir ? " he enquired of Holmes. " It's a bad business, with the old gentleman—that is to say the Italian gentleman who's been staying here—struck down as he has been. There's talk he may not live for much longer."

" I am the doctor," I corrected him, but said no more. It was obvious that the news of the Cardinal's death, or even certain knowledge of his identity, had not spread to the stable-yard, at any event.

The drive proceeded in silence. Neither Holmes nor myself wished to discuss the purpose of our visit in front of the coachman, and for my part, I was content to close my eyes and compose my nerves a little in preparation for what I was sure would be an ordeal on my part.

On arrival at the Hall, a servant arrived to carry Holmes' and my luggage, but I maintained my grip on my doctor's bag, and Holmes retained the Gladstone bag containing the tools peculiar to his trade. On our stepping into the hallway, we were greeted by a man who was obviously from his bearing the butler, Alvarez, who had been mentioned as the servant who had attended Cardinal Tosca and his secretary. His Spanish blood was evident in the set of his face and in the proud bearing with which he carried himself, and there was a look in his eyes that bespoke a considerable intelligence. However, remembering the description of his character that had been given to us earlier, there seemed to be something shifty, almost furtive, about his bearing and general demeanour.

" His Lordship will see you now," he said to us, and ushered us into a spacious drawing-room.

Lord Ledbury was a man of about sixty years of age, obviously still possessed of considerable energy and vitality. He advanced on Holmes and myself with his hand outstretched.

" Well, well, my dear fellow," he addressed Holmes. " It seems that we are fated to meet again in another complicated set of circumstances, are we not ? I fear that on the last occasion I rather resented your intrusion. Rest assured, though, that on this occasion I am delighted to see you. Since that last time, I have been following the cases in which you have been described by your friend John Watson—and you must be he," he broke off, advancing on me and wringing my hand warmly. " I must confess a sincere admiration for your methods. I was also unaware at that time of your connection with the other Holmes—by which I mean your brother Mycroft, of course—and I really must apologise for what must have seemed to you at the time to be insufferable rudeness. I do hope that you will be able to get to the bottom of this ghastly affair. Naturally, you will be staying as my guests until this whole horrible business has been cleared up."

The speech was delivered in the warmest possible tones, and appeared to me to be completely sincere. I was pleased to see that Sherlock Holmes received these sentiments most graciously, and expressed his pleasure at renewing the acquaintance of our host, and his gratitude for the hospitality that had been offered. I was relieved by this, as I knew that Holmes could at times neglect the social graces when engaged on a case; he had unwittingly been the cause of hurt feelings in the past—and it had been my thankless task to soothe those ruffled feathers.

" Before we investigate the scene, may I ask you a few questions ? " he asked Lord Ledbury.

" Indeed you may. I was expecting something along those lines." He broke off. " Ah, our tea," as a tray made its appearance. He waited until the servant had withdrawn. " Now, what is it that you wish to know ? "

" Firstly, where is Monsignor Mahoney at this moment ? "

" He is in his bedroom, to the best of my knowledge. Would you like me to have him called here ? "

" Not at present, thank you. Have you spoken to him since his return from London ? "

" I have not. I was merely informed that he had returned, and that he had retired to his bedroom."

" Very good. Could you tell me about the events of two nights ago ? That is, the night of the Cardinal's death."

Lord Ledbury seemed happy to do so, and his account corroborated that which had previously been given by Mahoney. He and his family had been driven to London for a function held in the early evening, and he had returned alone at about ten o'clock. His wife and daughters had remained in London, and had spent that night at the family's town house, where they were still.

" It is a fair drive from London, is it not ? "

" Somewhere in the region of two hours or a little more," his Lordship said, adding that on his return, the butler had immediately told him that he was to speak to Monsignor Mahoney, who in turn told him of the untimely death of the Cardinal.

" You entered the room and viewed the scene yourself ? " Holmes asked him.

" Indeed I did, and I sincerely wish that I had not. It is a scene that will haunt me to my dying day. There, at the head of my dining-table, in my family's dining-room, sat a corpse, shrouded in blood, a dagger protruding from its breast. That alone would be horrible enough, Mr. Holmes, but when you add to this the fact that the man was a prince of the Church, and my guest to boot, you may imagine my feelings."

" You have my sincere sympathy," said Holmes. " Certainly it is a circumstance that no man could wish to experience."

" Mahoney informed me that he had telegraphed your brother, and that he had spoken through the telephone to him. I had the instrument installed for my government work some years back, and though there are times that I regret its existence, I was grateful for its existence on this occasion."

" And you decided to leave the room in its original state, as Mahoney discovered it ? "

" Mahoney told me that your brother had so ordered it, as you would be investigating the matter."

" He was certainly premature in that assumption," said Holmes. " It was only a matter of a few hours ago that I first heard of the incident from him."

" It went against all my principles as a man and a

Christian, to leave the Cardinal there in that state, but given the importance and significance of his mission, and the orders from your brother, I could do no less."

" You are aware of the true reasons for the Cardinal's visit to this country ? My brother has informed me, by the way, and Watson here is also aware of them, so you may speak freely."

" Thank you. Yes, I am aware."

" And your feelings on the matter, if I may pry ? "

The peer sighed. " If you must, you must, I suppose. As you are probably aware, I am a Roman Catholic, as were my fathers and my ancestors before me. It has never occurred to me to change my religion and I may say, with all due modesty, that I am one of the foremost laymen of the Catholic Church in this country. However, I was aware of the Cardinal's mission to this country, and I must tell you that this was not to my liking." Holmes' eyebrows lifted in an expression of surprise, and the nobleman continued. " You may well consider it strange of me to say this, but I am above all an Englishman, and I believe that your brother and I would find ourselves in complete agreement regarding the probable state of this country were the highly placed person in question to declare his allegiance to Rome. For a member of the Government, such as myself, to profess his faith is enough to set the hounds of the popular press baying at his heels. For such a one as the man of who we speak to do so would plunge the nation into chaos. Brother would find himself set against brother, friend against friend. The situation would be intolerable."

" And yet you agreed to act as host to His Eminence during his stay here ? "

The peer sighed. " It was expected of me by the British government, in the form of your brother. He made the case to me most ably that it was better I than some hot-headed fanatic who would encourage Tosca in what was regarded by many as an act of folly. In addition, I have received an order of chivalry from the Vatican, and my hospitality would also be expected from that quarter."

" I understand your position. I will examine the dining-room presently, but before I do so, I must ask you two further questions. Firstly, do you have any suspicions as to who might have been responsible for the death of Cardinal Tosca ? "

" Why, it can be none other than Mahoney, can it ? Tosca was not the most forgiving of men when it came to others' faults, and I have heard him abusing Mahoney in such a fashion that had similar words passed between gentlemen, some sort of challenge might well have ensued."

" Do you seriously believe Mahoney to be capable of such an atrocious act ? "

" I tell you, Mr. Holmes, that I have seen his face after such admonishments, and it was the face of one who hates."

" Hates enough to kill ? " Holmes asked, half to himself. " I wonder."

" And your second question ? "

You have been informed of the letter that has vanished ? " The other nodded. " Do you have any idea where we might commence a search for it ? "

Lord Ledbury's face broke out in a broad smile. " I can do better than that," he informed Holmes. " I can present you with the letter itself. Come with me."

He led the way along a passageway to a room that evidently served as his study and library. Books lined the walls, and on examination it was clear that they were not merely ornaments, as in many great houses, but were well-thumbed works of reference on the subjects of law and international relations. One shelf was devoted to the works of modern philosophers and theologians, which also appeared to have been consulted regularly.

" I confess that I instructed my butler to abstract this document, which I considered to be of an inflammatory, not to say explosive, nature, while the Cardinal and Mahoney were eating their meal, and to give it to me at the earliest possible opportunity. On the night that His Eminence met his end, Alvarez went up to the room that His Eminence was using as his study, and presented the paper to me the next night."

" You had requested him to give you the paper as soon as possible. Why the delay ? "

" It proved impossible to effect the delivery any earlier. Mahoney, as you may have been told, appeared to be in a state of shock at the Cardinal's death, which I would now, after further consideration, put down to the effects of remorse. He required attention, and since Alvarez was the only servant who was aware of the situation, it was natural that he should be the one who attended Mahoney. Your brother arrived early the next day, and either I was obliged to be with him, or Alvarez was required to attend him for the duration of his visit. In any event, it was not until the evening of that day that I was able to secure the document."

" You have read it, of course ? "

The peer turned to Holmes, a look of shocked surprise upon his face. " Indeed I have not, Mr. Holmes ! It is not the place of a gentleman to read another's correspondence, especially one from such a personage as this."

" I fully appreciate your scruples in this matter," Holmes told him, " and I had no intention of accusing you. I merely felt that since you had some sort of official duties in regard to this affair, you might perchance have had occasion to view the document. My apologies if my words offended you."

" I take your meaning in regard to this matter. My apologies for the misunderstanding."

" In any event, you have done well to secure the letter in this way. It is good that it is no longer in what might be regarded by some as a dangerous location."

Holmes' words appeared to restore the peer's *amour-propre*. " Thank you. I felt it best that it be retained in a safe place. And here it is ! " He turned with a certain air of triumph, and revealed a safe fitted into the wall, which had been concealed behind a picture. He inserted a key attached to his watch-chain, and opened the door. " Here you are, Mr. Holmes, perfectly safe—."

He stopped, and turned to face us, his face ashen. " It has vanished ! " he informed us.

" Perhaps it is under some other papers in the safe ? " I suggested.

He turned back and frantically explored the contents of the safe. " No, it is not in the safe at all ! I placed it on the top of the pile of papers in the safe. I have a distinct memory of doing so, and of locking the safe afterwards. As you saw for yourselves just now, it was necessary for me to unlock the safe. It is not of the type that locks itself."

" May I examine the safe for myself ? " asked Holmes.

" You are welcome to do so, but I can assure you that the letter is not there."

Holmes stooped to the lock of the safe, and examined it through his lens in silence for a few minutes. " You have the only key, of course ? " he asked Lord Ledbury.

" Yes. That is to say, there are two keys; the one you saw

me use just now, which is always attached to my watch-chain, and a duplicate which is kept for safety in White-hall. As you are aware, I am no longer a member of the Cabinet, but I retain an office there for my remaining official duties."

" And that other key is in your office at this minute ? "

" I have no reason to believe otherwise. We can verify its existence by means of the telephone if you so desire." He shrugged, as if to indicate the futility of the operation.

" I do so desire," Holmes said to him. " It would be remiss of us not to do so."

" Very good." Ledbury touched a button, and in answer to the bell's summons, the butler entered, and was given instructions to connect the house with the Whitehall office. He departed on his errand, and Holmes turned to the nobleman.

" I notice your use of electricity for the bells in this house," he remarked.

" Ah, yes, a little crochet of mine. I feel that electricity, and matters electrical, will some day play a leading role in our everyday lives. For example, I am certain that the present unhealthy flames we presently use for illumination, be they of gas or tallow, will soon be replaced by electricity. See here," and he moved to a lever in the wall and pulled it. Instantly the room was flooded with a fierce light, and a loud hissing came from above our heads. Startled, I looked upwards, but was nearly blinded by the bright object suspended from the ceiling.

" A lamp of my own design," explained Ledbury. " I have hopes of improving it through my efforts. I have a small laboratory where I conduct experiments in order to perfect our lighting. Not all my experiments are successful, though..." He broke off as Alvarez entered and informed him that the connection to London had now been established. " This way, gentlemen," he instructed us as he strode out.

The telephone was housed in a small cabinet off the hallway, and Ledbury entered it, leaving the door open. " Kingsley ? " he barked into the mouthpiece. This was the first occasion on which I had seen a telephone in use, and I was fascinated to observe the process.

" Have the goodness to look in the second drawer on the left side, at the back," I heard Ledbury saying, followed in one or two minutes by " Then look again. It is never kept anywhere else." He turned to Holmes and myself with a worried expression. " The fool cannot locate it in its usual place." He withdrew a handkerchief from his pocket, and wiped his brow before holding the instrument to his ear once again, and listening with a face which betrayed extreme anxiety as the conversation progressed. " Then search every drawer—everywhere—and communicate with me as soon as you have located it," he snapped into the telephone before breaking the connection.

" I apologise," he said to us. " This should have been a simple matter, but it appears the key is not where I believed it to be. I am sure that Kingsley will make a competent search of the office, but in the meantime..."

" In the meantime, we could possibly assume that the thief has used the missing key to abstract the letter at some point between your placing it in the safe and now."

" Impossible ! " burst out the nobleman.

" It is not in the least impossible," Holmes corrected him. " Improbable, maybe, but as Watson here will inform you, one of my favourite dicta is that whenever you have eliminated the impossible, whatever remains, however improbable, must be the truth. There are, of course,

other possibilities that occur to me," said Holmes vague-
ly. " But let us deal with those in due course. What, may
I ask, would be your reaction to the suggestion that Alvarez might be responsible for the death of the Cardinal ? "

" Totally out of the question," retorted Ledbury. " He
may not have been in my employ for long, but I have never found him to be anything other than the perfect butler. Maybe some of his habits are not exactly those which
we might expect of an English butler, but that cannot be
laid at his door, after all, and there is no reason for me to
complain in these cases. But there is one very good reason
why I can tell you that it is most unlikely."

" That being ? "

" The fact that Alvarez, before he came to me, had at
some time in the past been part of the household of the
Cardinal in Spain."

" Given the reputation of the Cardinal's temper, and his
attitude to those serving him, that might seem like a possible motive, rather than an exculpation," Holmes objected.

" In this case, you would not think so, if you had seen
them together. I had occasion to mark the deference with
which he served His Eminence, and the change which
came over Tosca's face when the other was near him. Naturally, I realise that this is not guarantee of innocence, and
I realise how inconclusive it may sound, but that is my
opinion."

" Is Mahoney aware of this previous relationship ? "

" I fail to see how he could be ignorant of it."

" And yet he never mentioned it to us. Strange,
strange." He turned to face Ledbury " It is time that we
examined the scene of the murder."

" Very well," Ledbury answered, though he was obviously in considerable doubt regarding the recent events

concerned with the loss of the paper. He led the way through the Hall to a door which he attempted to open without success.

" By the by," asked Holmes, as we passed along the passageway, " maybe you can show us the general location of the offices of the house ? "

" The kitchen is that way through the green baize door," Lord Ledbury told us, pointing, " with the scullery beside it, and the laundry adjoining that."

" And the butler's pantry is there too, I take it ? " asked Holmes.

" As it happens, it is not. I am not sure of the reason for this, but the butler's pantry is in the general area of the room we are approaching, rather than in a more convenient and usual location by the kitchen."

" And these are the main stairs, I take it ? It would seem that it is possible for an observer on the landing to see someone exiting the kitchen area through the baize door. Please excuse me." Holmes abruptly left us, and bounded up the stairs to the landing, from where he looked down at us, craning his neck to and fro. " Thank you," he said on re-joining us. " I merely wished to verify something that had been told to us earlier."

" Very good," Lord Ledbury replied, who was obviously restraining his curiosity with regard to Holmes' actions. " Here we are at the door of the family dining-room, which I made available to His Eminence. This door at least is locked as it should be," he told us, extracting a key from his pocket and turning it in the lock. " I trust you are prepared, gentlemen."

CARDINAL PIETRO TOSCA

–

LEDBURY HALL

E stepped into the room, and I, for one, feared the worst. The sweet scent of the recently dead filled the room, but there was mercifully no smell of decay.

" What is this ? " cried Holmes. " We were told that the body had not been moved." He pointed to the dining table, on which lay the body of a large and powerfully built man, dressed in a scarlet cassock. The eyes of the corpse appeared to be bulging under their closed lids, as if in terror, and a look of fear suffused the face. One of the chairs, at the head of the table, had been pulled back a little, and the seat was lightly marked by bloodstains. A coffee service stood on a small side-table.

Ledbury's face turned pale, and he crossed himself. " I

have no conception," he cried. " I had given strict orders for this room to be sealed, and for no-one to enter. When I left this room last and locked the door, the Cardinal's body was sitting in that chair there." He pointed to the blood-stained chair with a hand that trembled.

" I must ask once more, how many keys exist to this room ? "

" This one here in my hand, and perhaps two or three others. In theory, it would be easy for anyone to take the key from the butler's pantry or the housekeeper's room, and to admit themselves. But the risk of being observed by any passer-by would have prevented that, I would have thought."

Holmes had been examining the carpet under the windows. " I fancy that our intruder did not use the door to enter and leave the room. I spy traces of soil here, and the faint indentations of footprints in the carpet. This type of casement window is much easier to open by a skilled practitioner than many householders care to believe. For example, it takes me less than ten seconds to effect an entry through a window such as this." He bent to examine the window frame. " Ah, as I suspected. The marks of a thin-bladed knife, such as I myself would use, should I ever have occasion to enter a room in this way. You will note that the catch of this window is not closed, while those of all the others have been secured. It is not possible to fasten such a catch from the outside."

" But who would do such a thing ? It is hardly desecration of a body. Indeed, it appears to be an attempt to secure some measure of dignity. I assure you, Holmes, that the sight of His Eminence sitting dead, with his eyes staring into the void, was a disturbing sight, to say the least of it."

" I agree with you that this seems to have restored a little decorum to the situation," remarked Holmes. " I notice also that the eyes have been closed. The situation is, however, more than a little extraordinary. You mentioned did you not, that when you locked the room, nothing had been moved from the position in which Monsignor Mahoney discovered it ? "

" That is correct."

" And the papers which were consulted by the Cardinal and Mahoney were where at that time ? "

" Why, on the table, of course." Ledbury appeared struck by this. " Is it possible that the body is now resting on those papers, since I do not see them there now ? "

" Possible, but unlikely, I feel. The same person who abstracted the letter from your safe is almost certainly he who is responsible for this act, and I am positive he would ensure that all the papers were in his possession. If I may be permitted to offer my surmise at this early stage, I would say that this room was visited first in the hope of encountering the letter, and the thief's attention was then turned to your study, after his failure to locate the letter he sought."

" It may well be as you say, Mr. Holmes. In any event, I feel we should move His Eminence from the table. I know that I will never be able to eat from it again. Vain superstition, I know, but..."

" Rigor should have departed by now," I told the other men, and confirmed this by taking hold of the dead man's left hand, which, as I had predicted, moved freely. As I did so, I noticed a peculiarity about the fingertips, but some instinct prevented me from mentioning it at the time.

As we moved the body to rest on the floor, where Ledbury had placed a folded tablecloth to act as a pillow, and another to act as a shroud, I became aware of the hilt of the paper-knife that Mahoney had informed us had been used to commit the murder. Since the dead man was dressed in his dark Cardinal's cassock with red piping, it was difficult to be sure of the matter, but it seemed to me that the volume of the bloodstains was substantially less than one might expect from a fatal wound of this type. Furthermore, although Mahoney had informed us that the wound had been delivered to the chest, the hilt of the dagger protruded from an area substantially lower than the chest, in an area which, from the experience of bayonet and knife wounds that I had gained in Afghanistan, rarely proved fatal, and was never capable of causing death in such a rapid manner as had been described to us. The expression of shock, almost of horror, that had been described to us was still present on the face, and it was with a sense of relief that I drew the sheet over the Cardinal's head.

After carefully laying the body to its position on the cloth and covering it, we turned our attention to the table, but as Holmes had foretold, there were no papers there, or indeed, elsewhere in the room.

As we searched, the voice of Alvarez could be heard outside, informing Lord Ledbury that there was a telephone communication from his Whitehall office, and that his assistant desired to speak with him. His Lordship made his excuses and left us.

" Holmes," I said to my friend as soon as we were alone and the door was closed. " I do not believe that Cardinal Tosca died as the result of that wound to the abdomen. I am not ignorant of these things."

Holmes said nothing, but raised his eyebrows.

" A wound like this, delivered to this area of the body, hardly ever results in death, unless it proceeds to a gangrenous state. I have never heard of a wound of this type being fatal in so short a time, unless it is accompanied by some other shock to the system"

" I lack your experience of the battlefield, but my scanty knowledge of anatomy persuades me that you are probably correct in your assumption that this is not a fatal injury."

" But there is more," I added. " Examine the fingers of the left hand."

Holmes raised the sheet and took the corpse's hand in his. " Well done indeed, Watson. The fingers, especially the middle and index fingers, appear to have suffered some sort of burn. Caused by a spirit lamp used to heat the coffee ? " He examined the coffee service and answered his own question. " No, that is not the answer. There is no such lamp such as one sometimes finds. It is interesting, though, that the Cardinal's cup is empty, and so is the coffee pot, while Mahoney's cup is still half-full."

" How do you know which is which ? "

" Elementary. We were told by Mahoney, if you will recall, that Cardinal Tosca took his coffee black. The cup which contained black coffee is empty, while the other, containing the beverage with milk added, is half-full. We may deduce that from the distribution of the grounds in the cup, the drinker of the black coffee was left-handed."

He examined the cadaver with a critical eye. " Let us see what the Cardinal has in his possession." He searched the dead man's garments, but failed to discover any object in the few pockets provided by the cassock. " Of course, at this point, we have no way of knowing whether there were indeed no objects in the pockets, or whether they have been removed. Undoubtedly, though, Tosca occasionally smoked a pipe, it would appear." He held out his hand, on the palm of which rested a few shreds of tobacco, which he smelt cautiously, and examined with his lens. " Were this a commonplace run-of-the-mill murder, I would hesitate to do this, but here..." He grasped the hilt of the dagger-shaped knife, and removed it from the corpse. " Well, well," he exclaimed softly.

I was forced to echo his amazement. The weapon which had allegedly killed Cardinal Tosca appeared to be little more than a toy. The blade was sharp enough for a paper-knife, but in my opinion too blunt to cut flesh, and the stiletto-like point likewise almost incapable of inflicting any serious wound. In addition, the blade was little more than two or three inches long. " That knife could never have served as the murder weapon," I confirmed.

" Nonetheless, Watson, the man is dead, and this was discovered in his body. It would seem foolish to discount the connection. Those burns that you discovered are almost certainly connected to his death, would you not say ? "

" It would seem likely, but what could have caused them ? I see no candles in this room. Indeed, this room appears to be lit by electricity, though the lighting here is of a different type to that we saw demonstrated in the study."

" These are incandescent globes, while what we saw in the study was obviously an arc lamp, albeit one of an unfamiliar and novel type."

At that moment Lord Ledbury re-entered the room, with a face that told of inner anguish. " I have just been speaking on the telephone with Whitehall," he told us. " I am persuaded that Kingsley has conducted a thorough search of my office there, and that the key I believed to be there certainly seems to have been removed. I think it would not be unreasonable to assume that this was the key used to open the safe and to remove the letter that I had placed there."

" Tell me," asked my friend. " Were any other items in the safe disturbed or removed ? "

" No, they were as I left them. The letter, though, was on the top of the pile of papers at the front of the safe."

" Which argues, would you not agree, that the prime object of the thief was the letter, and that the appearance of the letter was familiar enough to him that he need not search through the contents of the safe to find it ? "

" Possibly," the peer answered in an abstracted tone. " Forgive me, Mr. Holmes, but my mind is filled with anxiety. Do you realise that if this letter is made public, I will go down in history as the man who was chiefly responsible for the civil war of 1895 ? It is not a title I wish to hand down to posterity. If you have no objection, I would like to leave you and Dr. Watson and continue the search for the letter."

" If I may make a suggestion," Holmes addressed him, " I would recommend that you make arrangements with a local trustworthy undertaker who is able to keep all aspects of the matter quiet, requesting that the body be taken to the local hospital where it may be preserved with the minimum of formalities attached to the matter, until a post-mortem examination may be performed, if it is deemed necessary at some point, or it can be removed for burial."

" I believe that the firm of undertakers in the market town will be suitable for this purpose. I shall instruct Alvarez to provide them with the information."

" With respect, sir, I feel that this would be best arranged by yourself personally, by means of a written note, detailing some of the facts that we wish to be kept from the public, and making a strong request for secrecy in the matter. One of your outdoor servants could be employed to deliver the note."

" I take your meaning," said the nobleman. " I will attend to the business as you suggest." So saying, he left the room.

Holmes pursed his thin lips. " There are aspects to this case, Watson, that do not ring true to me, particularly in the matter of the letter. First, though, let us determine how the Cardinal met his end. Would you swear to it that the knife wound would not have killed him ? "

" I would swear to no such thing, but I would say it was extremely unlikely that that was the case. There may, of course, be another wound which we have overlooked." With some distaste, I bent to the body, and unbuttoned the cassock before examining the torso, but there was no sign of any other abdominal knife wound, or indeed of any other injury whatsoever.

" Let us summon Alvarez, and ask him some questions regarding the disposition of the body when he discovered it. I feel that his words may be of some value here." So saying, Sherlock Holmes moved to the electric bell, but stopped short before pressing it. " I have it ! " he exclaimed, bending to the bell-push, magnifying lens in hand. " See here ! " He offered the glass to me, and I peered through to examine the bell-push, but could detect nothing untoward, and I informed Holmes of this.

" The screws, man, the screws securing the brass plate to the wall. Do you not see that they have been removed and replaced recently ? Indeed, since the plate was last polished, since there is no polish remaining in the slots."

" What does this tell you ? " I asked.

" Let us see," he answered me, removing a small

screwdriver from his tool-kit and applying it to the screws. " Hah ! Even if it were not so clearly visible, the ease with which I can remove these indicates that they were recently disturbed. Excellent," he added, as the plate was removed. " Aha ! Yes, this is it, Watson. What would happen if I were to remove this wire here," he pointed with the screwdriver, but did not touch the wire itself, " and attach it to this screw here, which is obviously what has occurred recently ? "

" I cannot for the life of me tell you. Electricity and electrical apparatus appear as a sealed book to me."

" Then I will tell you. Whoever touches the plate would receive an electric shock through the part of the body touching the plate. Depending on the current and the potential, the electricity could deliver a powerful shock."

" I begin to see what you are driving at here. Would the shock be enough to kill ? "

" It could be so, but we should ascertain the details from Lord Ledbury. He seems to be very much *au courant* with the electrical system of this house, if you will pardon the feeble play on words. If the Cardinal suffered from a weak heart, even a relatively minor shock could prove fatal, however."

I considered what Holmes had said. " All this points in one direction, does it not ? "

" Indeed it does. There is only one man who would have the opportunity to— Ah, Alvarez," he broke off to address the butler, who had entered the room. " I wonder if you would be good enough to answer some questions."

" If I can be of help, I will attempt to answer as best I can, sir." There was a hint of a Spanish accent remaining in his speech.

" Good man. You served the meal to the Cardinal and to

Monsignor Mahoney on the night of the Cardinal's death, I believe."

" I did, sir. A light consommé, followed by saddle of lamb, with a coupe as dessert. I brought in the coffee with the dessert. Water was the only drink with the meal, though I believe that Monsignor Mahoney had taken a glass of sherry-wine before dinner."

" Did you notice the relationship between the two men while you were in the room ? "

" I noticed nothing untoward in that respect, sir. I could not hear their words, but they were saying little, and they were speaking in low voices." The butler's eyes kept flickering towards the white-wrapped form on the floor beside the table. I fancied I noticed a look of surprise on his features as he looked at the bare surface of the table and back towards the floor where the ghastly bundle lay.

" Yes ? " Holmes enquired, noticing the other's gaze.

" It seems to me, sir, that it is hardly decent for His Eminence to be lying on the floor in that way. Would it not be best if he were moved to a more appropriate place, such as the table ? "

" That is not for you to decide, Alvarez," Holmes told him sharply. " His Lordship is, I have every reason to believe, currently making suitable arrangements in this regard. He will no doubt issue you with your instructions when the details of this matter have been decided."

" Very good, sir." There was a flash of anger detectable in the man's eyes at this rebuke, but the tone of his voice remained civil.

" And after the meal the bell rang to summon you ? "

" That is correct, sir."

" You came to remove the coffee service ? "

" Why, no, sir." Holmes raised his eyebrows. " The bell

rang in my pantry, and I assumed that His Eminence was now ready for his second pot of post-prandial coffee. He was particularly partial to the coffee served in this house, sir, and it was usual for him to consume several servings of the beverage as a close to his evening repasts. I was carrying this second pot to the dining-room when Monsignor Mahoney's voice told me to wait outside, as His Eminence was unwell."

" And I suppose you have no way of knowing whether Monsignor Mahoney was in the dining-room at that time the bell rang ? "

" I happen to know that he was not, sir. As I left the pantry for the kitchen to order the coffee, I happened to catch sight of him on the upstairs landing."

" The obvious inference being that it was His Eminence himself who rang the bell. And how long did it take to prepare the coffee ? "

" A matter of five minutes or less. Cook is an intelligent woman and was anticipating His Eminence's wishes, based on the experience of previous evenings."

" But there was sufficient time for Mahoney to come downstairs and re-enter the dining-room while you were in the kitchen ? "

" Oh indeed, sir. No question about that whatsoever. After all, he must have done so, if he was on the landing when I left the pantry, and in this room when I returned here." Alvarez appeared to be puzzled by Holmes' question.

" Very good. Tell me, Alvarez, Lord Ledbury asked you to take a paper from the room used by His Eminence, did he not ? "

The butler licked his lips nervously. " That is not for me to say, sir."

" Lord Ledbury has informed me that this was the case. I merely wish to confirm a few details."

" In which case, sir, yes, he did."

" And you were able to locate the paper easily ? "

" Oh yes, sir. His Lordship had given me a precise description of the appearance of the letter."

" And you gave it to his Lordship at what time ? "

" On his return from London, on the evening of His Eminence's death."

" Did you indeed ? " mused Holmes. " And do you know the contents of the letter ? "

" I have no idea, sir. That is none of my business. I merely was informed by Lord Ledbury of the appearance of the envelope in which it was contained."

" Quite correct, Alvarez. Is there anything else that you would like to tell us ? "

" There is one small matter which may not be important, sir, but it seemed to me that as I heard the bell ring in my pantry, I heard a cry—perhaps more of a shriek—from the dining-room."

" Before or after the bell rang ? "

" I would have to say that it occurred at the same time, or at the most, a matter of a second or two after the bell."

" And did you attach any significance to this ? "

" I could not at the time, sir. But when I heard that His Eminence had experienced a seizure, it was then apparent to me that this must have been the cry he gave on suffering the stroke."

" I am sure that is the answer, Alvarez. By the way, do you understand the electrical system in this house ? "

For the first time in the interview, the butler smiled. " No, sir. I do not consider myself to be technically adept, and the whole business appears as a dangerous mystery to me. The whole of this electricity is His Lordship's hobbyhorse, if I may express it in those terms, sir. If you require any detailed knowledge, His Lordship will know, or I can send Bates, the handyman, to you if you would prefer."

" No, not at present," said Holmes, smiling. " But you had something to say to us ? "

" His Lordship wished me to inform you that dinner will be served in the main dining-room at half-past seven this evening, and particularly wished me to impress upon you that there will be no requirement to dress for dinner."

Holmes thanked the butler, who left us alone in the room, closing the door behind him. " Most interesting," Holmes remarked to me. " You noticed that his story did not precisely match that recounted to us by Ledbury as regards the delivery of the letter ? "

" I did indeed. He could be mistaken, of course."

" Indeed he could, but I do not consider it likely. The other point that I found to be of interest was his statement that he observed Mahoney when he left his pantry in answer to the summons by the bell."

" Yes, Mahoney told us the same, I recall."

" Methought at the time Mahoney did protest too much. It seemed to me that when he told us this, he was leaving a trail for us that we were meant to follow."

" Establishing to us that he was definitely not present when the Cardinal met his end ? "

" Precisely, Watson. There is another matter connected with this aspect of his story which we will discuss shortly." He glanced at his watch. " We still have half an hour before dinner. While we are waiting, would you care to assist me in a little experiment ? "

I assented, and he knelt in front of the bell-push, having

first drawn on a pair of stout leather gloves. He worked
with a screwdriver and some other tools for a few minutes,
from time to time passing me items to hold. At length,
he stood, and regarded the bell-push, which appeared un-
changed, with some satisfaction. " There, we are all set,"
he told me. " Be so good as to take this screwdriver by the
metal end, and press the bell-push using the wooden handle. Take care not to let your hand or any metal touch the
bell-push."

I did so, and instantly leaped back in amazement, drop-
ping the screwdriver, as a bright flash lit the room, and a
crackling spark leapt between the push and the plate surrounding it.

" You are not hurt, I trust ? " Holmes asked me.

My heart was pounding in my breast as I answered
him. To my astonishment, I found I was short of breath
as I spoke. " I am not physically hurt, but I am shocked
in my mind."

" And if you had pressed the push with your finger, you
would have been shocked in your body also," he commented. " Your finger would have suffered burns, and I am certain that your heart would have likewise been adversely
affected."

" I have seen in the journals that in America, some criminals are now executed using electricity. You think that
this is how Cardinal Tosca met his end ? "

" I am certain of it. The burns on his fingers, the expression on his face, what else could it be but death by
electricity ? "

" And the dagger ? Or rather, the paper-knife, as we
seem to agree that it was not capable of causing death ? "

" Let me reconstruct the scene for you. Before the meal
began, Mahoney found some occasion to enter the room

where the meal was to be served, and carried out the alteration that I performed just now. You saw for yourself that it took me a very short time indeed to carry out the work, and I have no reason to believe that Mahoney would have taken much longer. Once the meal had been served, the two prelates ate together, and it is quite possible that they were arguing during the course of the repast. We could ask Alvarez to confirm this, if we wished, but I see little point in our doing so, even if he is willing to speak, which I doubt. Mahoney was probably aware that Tosca would wish to work after the meal, and had laid his plans accordingly. As expected, he was asked to bring down papers, while Tosca waited here. He deliberately left some documents upstairs, and when Tosca noticed they were missing, he was sent upstairs, after words had passed between the two men. Note, however, that there is an inconsistency in the story that Mahoney told us in London."

" That being ? "

" He informed us that he was reprimanded by Tosca in front of Alvarez."

I cast my mind back. " He did indeed. But Alvarez has not confirmed this story."

" Indeed he has not, and it is Alvarez' version of events that I believe. If I were to be generous toward Mahoney— not a state of mind I feel inclined to adopt, I may say—I could assume that his reprimand in front of the servant took place on another occasion, quite possibly on the same evening. Being generous, let us say that his mind may have been confused on this point. So, let us assume that the coffee had been brought in before Tosca remarked the fact that the documents were missing, as we were informed.

" Mahoney than leaves the room, knowing that Tosca will finish the coffee and will ring for more, as he has done in the past. My guess is that he waited on the stairs for the sound of the electric bell, and the Cardinal's shocked cry, before placing himself in a location from where he could be seen clearly by Alvarez entering the butler's pantry."

" Thereby ensuring that he had an independent witness to verify that he was not in the room, should the Cardinal's screams be heard ? "

" Precisely that. Alvarez has just told us that a matter of a mere five minutes elapsed before the extra coffee was prepared and he brought it to the dining-room. You saw earlier how I went upstairs and came down again. Let us say that it takes one minute for Mahoney to make his way from the room where he was searching for papers back to the dining-room. This would mean that he spent all of four minutes searching for the missing paper before abandoning his quest. Less, if you consider that he also supposedly spent time in search of other papers."

" That is not a long time."

" Indeed it is not. I find it hard to believe that he would not have spent longer looking for that paper, especially following an expression of anger on the part of the Cardinal such as he described to us, should we choose to believe his story.

" The Cardinal was probably not killed outright, but made his way to the chair. We can never be certain of this, given the fact that the body has been moved. In any event, this was probably the Cardinal's last action before he slipped into unconsciousness or even death. Mahoney brought down the papers, in order to add verisimilitude to his story, and discovered his master, shocked into unconsciousness, if not actually dead, as I say. We may make further enquiries if we choose, but I would be reasonably certain that Tosca suffered from a weak heart. Especially if he was in the habit of fasting, it is reasonably certain that the shock administered by the electric bell would be sufficient to incapacitate him permanently. I have no doubt that Mahoney knew of the Cardinal's weakness and arranged matters accordingly. He is almost certainly the prime mover behind the Cardinal's death. In any event, with the documents he brought with him from downstairs, he also brought the paper-knife, which he plunged into the Cardinal's lifeless body in an attempt to divert investigation from the true cause of his death."

I shuddered. " Holmes, this is horrible to think of."

My friend nodded in agreement. " I fear we are dealing with a man who is somewhat deranged. I think it is fair to assume that if the Cardinal was not dead at this point, the shock of the stabbing would deliver the *coup de grâce*, though as you point out, the wound itself would be insufficient to cause death. Having ensured the Cardinal's death, it would be a simple matter for him to keep Alvarez from entering the room, and to restore the bell to its former state. As you saw, however, it was obvious to an attentive observer that there had been some tampering carried out."

" Obvious to you, maybe, Holmes," I said, " but I doubt if there is another man in the nation who would have remarked it."

" Be that as it may, the fact of his being a priest gave Mahoney the opportunity to sit alone and to remove all traces of suspicion from the room until Ledbury's return. Who knows what awful thoughts went through his mind in those hours ? If Tosca was not dead, the waiting for the final gasp must have been appalling and nerve-racking in the extreme."

" It is almost impossible for me to believe that one who

is supposedly a man of God, could have committed such a foul act ! " I exclaimed.

" They are human, like the rest of us frail mortals," my friend remarked, shaking his head. " Mahoney gave us a motive for his act, did he not, when he described his humiliations at the hands of the Cardinal."

" It seems so—so petty," I said.

" Most murders are committed for the most trifling of reasons. Murders for grand motives which you or I might consider to be worthy of the crime, if I may put it that way, are few and far between, relatively speaking."

As he finished speaking, we heard the noise of the dinner-gong.

" We should at least wash," I said to Holmes, " even though we have been instructed not to dress for dinner."

" Very well," he agreed, and we left the fatal chamber.

Mycroft Holmes

—

Whitehall, London

N our arrival in the dining-room, we discovered Lord Ledbury standing by the sideboard, a glass of sherry in his hand.

" I do realise that the circumstances are somewhat out of the ordinary," he said to us by way of greeting, " but that is no reason to dispense with the usual trappings of a civilised life. A glass for you gentlemen while we await Monsignor Mahoney ? "

We both accepted, and we returned the toast of our host. While I sipped my wine, I was concerned with how we would be able to exchange civil conversation and break bread with a man whom Holmes had determined to be a cold-blooded murderer. Lord Ledbury was pleasant enough in making small talk with Holmes and myself, but it appeared that he was impatient for the arrival of his other guest. At length he pulled out his watch, and frowned at it.

" The man must be asleep," he grumbled, reaching for the bell. A minute later, Alvarez entered. " Please inform Monsignor Mahoney that we await his company," Ledbury instructed the butler. He turned to us. " Another glass while we wait ? "

He replenished our glasses from the decanter, but we were fated never to taste our drinks. Alvarez came into the room, red-faced and panting.

" Excuse me, sir," he said to Ledbury, " but there's no sign of the Monsignor. He is not in any of the rooms upstairs, and it seems as though some of his luggage has gone from his room."

Holmes let out an exclamation of annoyance, and Lord Ledbury turned to look at him.

" You may go, Alvarez," Holmes told him, and when he had gone, addressed Lord Ledbury. " Pardon me, sir, for my abrupt dismissal of your servant, but I did not wish to discuss this matter in front of him."

" You intrigue me, Holmes. This is becoming a house of mysteries, is it not ? "

" One mystery is solved, I feel," Holmes told him, and proceeded to lay out his deductions regarding the death of Cardinal Tosca. Lord Ledbury listened in near silence, interrupting with an occasional question that showed he was following the account with complete attention.

" So a murderer has flown the coop, has he ? Well, he cannot have gone far. I can call the local constabulary, and they will watch every railway station, visit every inn and public house where he may choose to stay. We will soon have the man, do not fear."

Holmes shook his head sadly. " I hope you are correct, but I fear you may be mistaken there. We should summon the servants and question them as to whether any of them witnessed his departure. Dinner must wait."

After the indoor servants had been questioned, to no avail, those of the outdoor servants who had not departed for the night were summoned. To our amazement, the groom who had driven Holmes and myself from the station calmly stated that he had carried Mahoney to the station.

" He told me that he had received a telegram from London and he had to catch the next train."

" What was he carrying ? " Holmes asked.

" A small Gladstone and a case for documents. He was hanging on tight to the document case all the way to the station. He seemed nervous, and he kept asking me to hurry up."

" And did you see which train he caught ? "

" Yes, sir, it was the 5:25 express to King's Cross."

Holmes and Ledbury looked at each other with an air of disappointment. " Thank you, Fergus," said Ledbury.

" Our pigeon is well and truly flown," remarked Holmes with an air of dejection. " There would seem to be little use in your calling out the constabulary, I fear. There is no reason for us to blame that coachman, though. He had no reason, after all, to suspect that anything was amiss. However, I must contact brother Mycroft at the Diogenes and inform him of events. At least, locating a Monsignor should be a simple matter, even in the metropolis, after Mycroft has passed the word to the appropriate authorities."

" Provided always that Mahoney continues to wear the insignia of his calling," added Lord Ledbury dourly. Of the two men, he seemed the more downcast by events. " Do you assume," he asked Holmes, " that he has the letter with him ? "

" I can assume nothing else," answered Sherlock Holmes. " If the letter is not here, and Mahoney is also absent, then it would seem logical to deduce, would it not, that the letter is in his possession. Come, let us use the telephone to speak with brother Mycroft."

Following Lord Ledbury's performance of those rites which seemed necessary to establish communication with the Diogenes Club, he handed the instrument to Sherlock Holmes, who seemed to enter conversation with one of the Club servants. At length, with an expression of disgust, he handed back the instrument to Ledbury.

" It appears that Mycroft is not at the Club," he told us. " Can you connect us to his Whitehall office ? "

The peer shook his head. " At this time of night, the employee who operates the telephones will have left the building. There will be no way of making such a connection."[*]

" In which case, sir, Watson and I must forego dinner here—a circumstance which affords me no pleasure, I can assure you—and return to London by the earliest possible train. If you would be kind enough to request the groom

---

[*] Editor's note: It has been a minor mystery to many Sherlockians why Sherlock Holmes failed to avail himself of the telephone, given his enthusiastic adoption of other forms of technology that made their appearance during the period of his activity. As we know, he preferred the telegram, but Watson records no reason for his disdain for the more modern method of communication. Maybe this riddle will be clarified and solved in some later adventure yet to be discovered in the deed box or dispatch-box.

to harness the trap, it would be much appreciated."

" I will do that," answered Lord Ledbury, reaching for the bell, " and I will also order that sandwiches or some such refreshment be prepared for your journey. I am sorry to be deprived of your company tonight."

Holmes smiled. " I am sure that we will return soon," he assured Ledbury.

The trap was soon harnessed and we were lucky to find an express train leaving for London within ten minutes of our arrival at the local station. Seated alone in our first-class compartment, and devouring the sandwiches that had been provided for us, Holmes turned to me with a worried expression.

" I have failed badly here, Watson," he confessed to me.

" You appeared to be less concerned when we were at Ledbury Hall."

" Alas, that was for outward show alone. Vanity, vanity, all is vanity, is it not ? With you, Watson, I can reveal my inner self to an extent that has not been possible for me in the past. You have the *air sympathique*, as our French cousins would have it, which makes it a positive pleasure to set forth my inner feelings."

I was flattered that Holmes should consider my company to be of such value to him, and settled back with a glass of the excellent Burgundy, a half-bottle of which had been packed along with the sandwiches.

" I have failed, Watson," Holmes repeated to me. " It is not merely a question of the damage to my personal pride, though I confess that is perhaps more of a blow than it should perhaps be, but also the fact that so much hangs on the successful resolution of this case. On a national level, this could be a disaster for the country should the letter be made public, and the contents be as explosive as we have been led to believe. Also, and I will freely agree that this is of lesser national consequence, there is the matter of my relationship with my brother."

" That being ? "

" As you can see, he is my elder, and I freely recognise his superiority in certain matters. However, I am highly conscious of the fact that he has depended on me to solve this problem. Future relations between us could become strained, I fear, if this matter is not settled."

It was rare for Holmes to unburden himself in this manner, and I was sensible of the fact as I endeavoured to reassure him. " There can be no doubt that you will discover the answer," I told him.

" It is not the discovery of the answer that worries me. The merest beginner in the craft could have discovered what I have done. It is the fact that Mycroft depends on me to be the actor, rather than the thinker in our family. And in this case I have failed him. I should have foreseen that Mahoney would divine our purposes, and would attempt to evade us. The fact that I failed to do so is inexcusable in my own eyes and will, I fear, be inexcusable in his as well." With this, he threw himself back into his seat, and placed his unlit pipe between his teeth. I started to reply, but he waved his hand in my direction. " Do not speak, Watson. Your silence is a consolation in itself." So saying, he closed his eyes, and remained motionless for at least ten minutes, during which time I applied myself to the wine.

Suddenly he addressed me, without, however, opening his eyes. " There is, however, something which gives me considerable pause for thought, and which may well lead us to a successful conclusion."

" Are you referring to the discrepancy that we noted

earlier between Lord Ledbury's account of the acquisition of the letter, and that of Alvarez ? "

Sherlock Holmes' face, which hitherto had assumed an expression of despondency, took on a new animation at these words, and he sat up and opened his eyes. " Precisely, Watson. You have hit the spot with unerring accuracy. Either Lord Ledbury or his butler has not told us the truth regarding this matter. The questions we must ask ourselves are firstly, which one has given us the true account, and secondly, to what end is the other one providing us with false information ? "

" Is it likely that the confusion is the result of an honest mistake on the part of one of the parties involved ? " I suggested.

" I think this to be improbable, given the importance of the matter, but it is obviously a possibility that we cannot entirely discard. We are nearly there," he added, after a glance out of the train window.

I packed away the remainder of our rough dinner, and as the train came to a halt in the London terminus, followed Holmes through the fog to the cab rank, where we hailed a hansom to take us to the Diogenes Club. " Even if he was not there earlier, I cannot imagine that he will miss his nightly visit there," Holmes told me, referring to his brother Mycroft.

He was proved correct when, on arrival at the Diogenes Club and giving our names to the porter, we were admitted to the presence of Mycroft Holmes, whose face was set in stern lines.

" Well, Sherlock," he said to my friend in tones that matched his countenance. " What brings you here ? I had imagined you to be still at Ledbury. Have you solved the case so quickly ? "

" I fear not," said his brother, in abashed tones. He related what we had discovered regarding the movement of the body, and the almost certain fact that the Cardinal had been killed through the electric bell, rather than the dagger that had been discovered. He then passed to the letter, and the two different accounts that we had received of its retrieval, followed by its disappearance, and the flight of Mahoney. As he proceeded, Mycroft Holmes' face took on a dark expression. At the end of Sherlock Holmes' recital of the events, there was a ponderous silence, which lasted for a good two or three minutes. At length Mycroft Holmes heaved himself to his feet, towering over his seated brother, and spoke.

" I am disappointed in you, Sherlock. I had expected more from you than this. Yes, you have done excellently in discovering the cause of death, and in identifying the killer. There is no doubt that you have achieved much in this regard. I suppose," he sighed, " that you cannot be held to be at fault in allowing the letter to disappear from the safe at Ledbury, though I naturally expect you to discover the means by which it vanished, and the perpetrator. Allowing Mahoney to escape, however," and here his voice took on a sharper tone, " was inexcusable. The man is a menace to this country."

" On account of the letter that he has in his possession ? " I asked.

" On account of who he is, Doctor," Mycroft Holmes informed me. " I was anxious for Cardinal Tosca to make this visit to England at least in part because I knew that he would be accompanied by Mahoney."

" I fail to understand what you are saying here."

" Monsignor Mahoney is a known Fenian of the deepest dye. One of those who will agitate for Home

Rule—between ourselves, I do not consider that to be a bad thing in itself—but Mahoney has links to those who will stop at nothing to achieve their ends. For a man of the cloth, he associates with men who are themselves associated with violence—that is to say, they are men who seek to overthrow the government of this land by force of arms and revolt. I do not say that he himself is guilty of violence, but we know—and I cannot provide further details to you at this juncture—that he plays a central role in the organisation."

" Why did you not tell us of this earlier ? " asked Sherlock Holmes.

" It was not considered necessary for you to know," his brother answered him shortly.

" You mean that you did not think it worth your while to tell me," my friend said, with some warmth in his voice.

" Not I alone, Sherlock," was the reply, given in a softer tone of voice. " The Home Secretary, the Prime Minister and I all agreed that the knowledge of Monsignor Mahoney's links with these hooligans should be kept to the smallest number possible. But it was my hope that by observing him and his doings, we would be able to uncover more of the nest of vipers. Ledbury Hall was chosen for the reasons that you have been informed of, as well as for its relative isolation, which would enable us to take careful note of any visitors."

" Does Lord Ledbury know of any of this ? " I could not refrain from asking.

Mycroft Holmes gave a bitter laugh. " Naturally he knows nothing. It was not considered necessary for him to know. Before setting the hounds after the vanished Mahoney, though, we have a more urgent task ahead of us. That is, we must inform the public of the death of the

Cardinal. He had made himself a little more visible in the British public's eye than we would have wished, and his sudden disappearance from the public stage may raise a few eyebrows."

" Then I would suggest that we continue with the fiction that he suffered some sort of apoplectic fit which resulted in his death. If you wish me to make a public announcement to that effect, I will do so, and Watson here will provide the medical backing to the story."

" Your name and that of Dr. Watson here would no doubt add considerable verisimilitude to the story," mused Mycroft. " I will also add that Tosca died in a hotel, rather than at Ledbury Hall. It will avoid some questions, and will also divert any possible unwelcome attention away from Ledbury. In addition, I feel it would be as well to have an official police statement, to still any remaining doubts."

" I leave that to you to arrange." It was plain to me that Sherlock Holmes was a little offended by his brother's suggestion.

" Is there any police officer in particular whom you feel could handle this task to advantage ? "

Sherlock Holmes was prompt in his response. " Inspector Stanley Hopkins. He has intelligence and discretion. If you involve him in this matter, he will be brought to the attention of his superiors, and that would be no bad thing for his career. He is one of the few Scotland Yard detectives whom I would like to see advanced in the force."

" Very well," answered his brother, making a note in a small book. " I will ensure that he is assigned to the case, and will be available to assist you in your pursuit of Mahoney and the letter."

" Are there not special branches in the official

departments who should be chasing Mahoney ? " I asked him. " Is it not somewhat unreasonable for you to be asking your brother to do this work ? "

" There are indeed such departments within the police force, and within other organs of the government," Mycroft admitted. " However, there are too many of them for comfort, and they often seem to bear a greater animosity towards each other than they do towards their assigned adversaries. No, in this case it is definitely better that Sherlock is assigned to the task. Given the current state of the Home Office, not to mention the personal wishes of the Prime Minister and His Holiness, my brother must lead the investigation. Believe me, Sherlock," he said, turning to his brother, " though I may be less than delighted at the current turn of events, you should not look on this task in any way as being retribution for sins of omission or commission. I know you well enough that I need not stress further the importance of this whole affair. We are all eagerly awaiting the return of the letter, as you know. And if Mahoney is captured into the bargain, Her Majesty's Government will be well pleased with the situation."

" Very good, " his younger brother answered him. " Rest assured that I will do all I can to settle things as quickly as possible."

" And discreetly," added Mycroft Holmes in a stern tone. " Doctor, I need hardly remind you that this is one of Sherlock's cases which is not to be mentioned in public."

It was a novel experience for me to see Sherlock Holmes, usually as self-assured a man as one could wish to meet, shrink into himself under the sting of his brother's words. " Very good, Mycroft," he mumbled. " Come, Watson."

" This is a pretty situation," he grumbled to me as we

made our way down Whitehall, almost deserted at this time of night. " It is all very well for Mycroft to offer me Hopkins as an assistant, but in a case like this, where a man has gone to earth in the warren of the metropolis—and we cannot even be sure that he has done that—it is a small army that is required, not one man with no connection to the special branches of the police dealing with these matters, however capable he may be as an individual."

" It is hard to know where to start," I agreed.

" As always in such cases, one starts from the beginning," retorted Holmes. " We will make our way back to Ledbury and seek out whatever clues are to be found there."

" Tonight ? " I asked, somewhat incredulously.

" Indeed. I believe that we will be in good time for the last train from King's Cross if we do not dawdle on the way."

" And leave Mahoney to run around London ? "

" I have a strong suspicion, my dear Watson, that he is the least of our problems. He has become, if I am not wholly mistaken, an embarrassment to his colleagues in the movement of which he is a member. It would not surprise me in the least were his body to be discovered floating in the Thames, or in some dark and forgotten alleyway within the next few days."

" Holmes, you shock me. Do you really believe that his associates would do such a thing ? "

Sherlock Holmes shook his head gravely. " Consider this," he said to me. " These groups wish to preserve their secrecy. If Mahoney is sought by the authorities, all of the gang may be in danger of discovery. And if he is captured, the risk of his betraying his comrades to their enemies becomes much greater, does it not ? It is therefore simpler for them simply to dispose of him."

The matter-of-fact way in which Holmes casually described the murder of a fellow human being sent a shiver through me. " You seem very sure of this. Will Mahoney himself not have considered this, however ? "

" It is quite likely," admitted Holmes. " But he is one, and they are many. I do not give much for his chances, especially as Mycroft has no doubt set a watch on the ports, and it will be impossible for him to leave the country."

" And the letter ? Do you not consider that he will be carrying it with him ? "

Again my friend shook his head. " If Mahoney has the brains for which I give him credit—and he is by no means a stupid or foolish man—he will have secreted the letter in a place where he can use it to preserve his life. That letter means more to his group than almost any other object on this earth. If he can persuade the other members that he is the only one in possession of the knowledge of its whereabouts, it is possible that he may save his life, albeit temporarily."

I shuddered. " And you feel that the letter may be at Ledbury still ? "

" I consider it more than likely."

" But we were told that he was carrying a document case when he left," I protested.

Holmes considered this, but only briefly. " Bluff, Watson, mere bluff, I consider."

We had by this time reached the station, and as Holmes had foretold, there was a train departing for Ledbury in a few minutes. We purchased first-class tickets, and settled ourselves in a compartment. I took up my end of the conversation.

" How much, do you consider, did Cardinal Tosca know

of his secretary's political leanings ? " I asked Sherlock Holmes.

" That, my dear Watson, is a very interesting question. It is quite possible, is it not, that the Cardinal had discovered somehow that his secretary was involved in this business, and had threatened to expose him ? Maybe he had even threatened to remove him from the priesthood as a consequence." Having said which, he added, " We have work before us, Watson," and closed his eyes, seemingly falling asleep instantly. For my part, my mind raced through the fantastic possibilities and the task that lay before us, and I was unable to obtain any rest until we reached Ledbury station.

Señor Juan Alvarez

–

Ledbury Hall

E arrived at Ledbury Hall a little after eleven o'clock, having persuaded the village carter to convey us from the station, Holmes rewarding him generously for his service. Alvarez, the butler, opened the door in answer to our ringing the bell, with a look of complete astonishment on his face. From his appearance, he had obviously thrown on his coat hurriedly, and his speech was a little slurred, leading me to believe that he had been drinking.

" I believed you gentlemen to be in London, sir," he addressed Holmes. " His Lordship gave me to understand that that was the case. I am afraid that his Lordship has retired for the night. If you wish, however, I could wake him, should you desire to speak with him."

" No, no, Alvarez," Holmes informed him in that easy manner of his. " There is nothing that requires his Lordship's urgent attention."

" I am not sure that your beds have been properly aired. I will wake the housekeeper immediately and see to it, though." He turned as if to move away, but Holmes put a strong hand on his shoulder.

" There is no need for that. There is work for Doctor Watson and myself to be done, and I doubt very much whether we will require a bed tonight." As Holmes spoke these words, I fancied that I saw a look of surprise and worry pass over the man's face, but it disappeared as quickly as it had arrived, and I could not be certain that I had, in fact, seen it.

" Very good, sir. May I bring you some refreshment ? "

" That will not be necessary, thank you."

" May I ask where you wish to perform your work, sir ? I should perhaps inform you that the local firm of undertakers removed His Eminence's body some hours ago." His voice was formal and a little distant, and Holmes adopted a similar tone when replying.

" Thank you for that information, Alvarez. I propose to start in the rooms which were occupied and used by Monsignor Mahoney and his late Eminence. Perhaps you will be good enough to lead us to them ? "

" Very good, sir. Please follow me." He led the way up the stairs to a door at the end of the passage. " The three rooms that may be reached through this door, consisting of two bed-rooms and one sitting-room, form a self-contained suite of rooms. The arrangement of the rooms was made for his present Lordship when he was younger, I am given to understand."

" Out of interest, Alvarez, how long have you been in Lord Ledbury's service ? " Holmes spoke almost nonchalantly, but I could sense that the answer to the question held some importance in Holmes' eyes.

" A matter of some a few months, sir."

" And prior to that ? "

" It is not my place to discuss such matters, sir."

" Come now." Holmes spoke with some asperity. " You know well on what business I am engaged here, and I am sure that you are well aware of some of the implications of the events that have taken place in this house over the past few days."

The butler swallowed nervously. " I held the position of head footman at the household of His Eminence in Rome for a number of years before coming here. I had held a similar post in the household of His Eminence when he held the title of Archbishop of Toledo."

" Thank you, Alvarez."

We entered the sitting-room which had been used as a study by Tosca and Mahoney. Since we had been informed that Mahoney had departed Ledbury Hall with a document case in his hand, and also taking into account the fact that there had been a considerable number of papers on the dining-room table which had apparently vanished, I was not expecting many papers to remain, but I was mistaken. There was an untidy stack of papers on the small occasional table, upon which Holmes pounced like a tiger on its prey, furiously scanning the sheets and tossing them aside with an expression of disappointment as he failed to locate what he was seeking.

" I should have anticipated that such a document would be well hidden," he remarked. He took in the mass of deed boxes and other containers stacked beside a bureau. " If

Mahoney has really left the fatal letter here, the perfect hiding-spot would be here, in one of these."

" I fail to grasp your meaning. Surely this would be the first place one would attempt a search ? "

" If he were to hide the letter among all the other papers here, most searchers would abandon the quest in disgust before even attempting to find it."

" I agree, it appears to be an impossible task."

" Hardly that," smiled my friend, pulling the ever-present lens from his pocket, and bending to examine the first of the boxes, before stopping to examine the next. " Ha ! " he exclaimed suddenly, after he had examined some six or seven containers. " I think we may be relatively certain that it is one of these two here." He tugged at the lid of one of the boxes he had indicated, but to no avail. " No matter," he remarked, drawing out his picklocks. After a minute or so, the box lid flew open at his touch, to reveal a pile of papers. " Here, do you take these," he ordered me, presenting me with the sheets at the top of the pile, " and I will search through the remainder."

I was puzzled by how Holmes expected us to recognise the letter for which we were searching, and mentioned this to him.

" In this case, Watson, it would appear to be a case for dedication rather than inspiration. We must examine every document and the contents of every envelope. It is not without the bounds of possibility that he has filled another envelope with the letter."

I felt a little uneasiness at this examination of another's correspondence and private papers, albeit in the service of my country. Holmes, however, appeared to be displaying no such scruples, and was soon engaged in rapidly scanning the papers in his hand, and laying the discarded papers to one side. I followed his lead, but was unable to locate any document which bore a resemblance to that which had been described to us.

I could not help but remark the contents of some of the papers that passed before my eyes. Even now, it would be injudicious in the extreme to detail their contents. I can only say that Cardinal Tosca was involved in an astonishing variety of activities, involving the governments of most European nations. As I laid the last of the papers on the table, Holmes spoke.

" Indeed, Watson. I have been watching your expression as you have been looking through these papers, and I can only say that I am as amazed as you. I had no idea that Tosca had his fingers in all these pies. Strictly speaking, I would say that these papers are still the property of the Church, but I think it behooves us to make my brother aware of the matters contained in them. Still, we may be sure that the letter we seek is not in this box. Let us try the other." So saying, he positively flew at the other box he had previously indicated, and in a matter of a few seconds had opened it. " Here," he ordered brusquely, presenting me with a fresh collection of documents.

After a search through the box, at the very bottom, I came across an envelope which appeared to be of unusual quality and thickness. On opening it, I extracted a document, handwritten in the Italic hand of a master of the art on a heavy laid paper, which, while not precisely that for which we were searching, nonetheless appeared to be of more than a little relevance. It bore the device of the Holy See at the top of the page, and was written in Latin, a language with which I was (and still am) less familiar than perhaps I should be (save for the medical terms I encountered in my profession). A heavy wax seal was appended.

As a result of my being unable to read the Latin, I passed the letter to Holmes, who appeared to be reading it with the same degree of fluency as he could read a document written in our English tongue.

" Well, Watson, this is not the document we have been seeking, but it is one of great interest to us, nonetheless. Indeed, it is even more dangerous to the security of this nation. This document, prepared by the highest authorities in the Vatican itself, is an expression of intent between the Church of Rome and the British Crown. On the succession to the throne of the person in question, the Church of Rome will become the official religion of this nation. There are spaces for the seal and signature of the Royal personage involved. The seal and mark of the Holy See are already present. We may take it that Tosca's mission was to obtain the written consent of the Royal personage, following which, this country would automatically fall under the leadership of the Bishop of Rome on the accession of the signatory. There would be no room for equivocation. This document is explicit."

" This is quite incredible, Holmes ! If this came to pass, the country would be engulfed in flames ! "

" I question your melodramatic metaphor, but I fear that you are substantially correct there."

" What will you do with this ? "

" It is a matter for Mycroft, is it not ? This document should be taken to him in Whitehall as soon as is possible."

" Together with the letter that he mentioned and which we are still seeking ? "

" Naturally. Of course, this document is of the utmost importance, but the letter likewise is of significance. We must find all relevant documents."

We redoubled our search of the boxes Holmes had

previously indicated, but to no avail.

" I had deduced that these boxes we have just searched are the last to have been opened, as is evident by the disturbance of the dust and the state of the locks. However, it is just within the limits of possibility that I may have missed some clue as to the state of the other boxes. Come, let us search them as well."

The other boxes soon yielded to Holmes' skill with the picklocks, and we ransacked their contents, but our efforts bore no fruit.

" Surely we should continue to search these rooms, nonetheless ? " I suggested. " These boxes are, after all, only one of the places in which we might discover the letter."

" We should indeed search the whole of the rooms. Who knows what other valuable clues we may come across ? "

A thorough search of the rooms yielded a number of interesting objects, including a revolver in the room previously occupied by Mahoney, which we discovered between the bed and the wall. This weapon, as Holmes remarked to me with a smile, was not the kind of property that one would expect to find in a clergyman's bedroom.

" However, if, as you say," I observed to Holmes, " he has quit Ledbury Hall to meet his confederates, who may be of a somewhat hasty and violent temperament, it would seem strange that he has left this behind him."

" His leaving it here may not be entirely intentional. Recall that he left the house in a hurry, fearing to be discovered. He would almost certainly have seized those objects that were closest to hand, and which would have provided him with the most safety. Note, though, that the original letter has yet to make its appearance."

We also discovered a pair of spectacles, in a case which bore the name of a optician's shop in Rome. On examining these, holding them to his own eyes and peering through them, Holmes declared them to be reading glasses. " It is clear that he required these in order to do any paperwork, judging by the lenses."

" In which case, he may well feel the need to visit an optician in order to procure a replacement," I suggested. " In that event, it should be possible for us to keep watch on all such shops, and have him apprehended when he makes an appearance."

Holmes shook his head. " I fear that would be a somewhat impractical course of action. There are literally hundreds of such shops in London alone, and we have no information that he will be in the metropolis. We should not overlook the possibility, though, that he may have another pair of spectacles with him. However," noticing my somewhat downcast expression and clapping me on the shoulder, " this is certainly the kind of thinking that may well bring about results. Who knows what little mistake he may make in the future that will lead to his apprehension? It is my experience," added Holmes, " that in the overwhelming majority of cases, criminals believe themselves to be of superior intelligence and possess greater foresight than the average. Happily for society, but unhappily for them, they are almost invariably mistaken in these beliefs."

" That may well be," I answered him. " But what is our next step ? "

" In the morning, we must make one more search for the missing letter, and any additional clues that he may have left behind. This time, we should not restrict ourselves to these rooms, but I fear it will be fruitless. Following this, we should return to London, inform Hopkins of the progress of the case, and request him to send his myrmidons forth throughout the metropolis in the search for Mahoney. Mycroft must then be informed of the developments here, and I will relinquish the case to the official force with the greatest pleasure. I had no wish to be involved originally, and it is solely on account of Mycroft that I am at all connected with the case."

Accordingly, we made ourselves as comfortable as possible, Holmes on the bed that had been used by Tosca, and I on that which had been occupied by Mahoney. Early in the morning, we arose and presented ourselves to a somewhat astonished Lord Ledbury. To my surprise, Holmes did not mention the fact that we had discovered the document that I had discovered, but merely requested permission to search the Hall for the missing letter, which was granted. As Holmes had foretold, we were unable to locate the missing letter, and the search failed to reveal anything that might shed light on the present whereabouts of Mahoney. Accordingly, we returned to London, after Holmes had instructed Ledbury to say as little as possible about the recent events, and to inform his servants to do the same.

" Do you wish me to visit Mycroft with you ? " I asked Holmes as we reached King's Cross station.

" At this juncture, I think it is best if I alone beard the lion in his den," Holmes replied. " Your offer of support is greatly appreciated, I assure you, but I would not wish to expose you to Mycroft's temper, which is considerable on such occasions, I can assure you from past experience." He managed a thin smile. " If you will have the goodness to make your way to Baker-street and instruct Mrs. Hudson to prepare a nourishing luncheon, you will have done your duty and more."

I did as he requested, and waited his return with some interest. A little after midday, Sherlock Holmes returned, and flung his hat into a corner.

" I know you mean well, but do not address me, I beg you, Watson, until I speak to you again," he said, short-ly. " I am in the worst of tempers, and I have no wish to bite a hand which wishes me only well, as I know do you."

So saying, he flung himself into his armchair, and filled his clay pipe with the cheap shag tobacco that he affected, lighting it and smoking it furiously until it was exhausted, before flinging it into the fireplace where it shattered.

" I am now in somewhat of a state to entertain conversa-tion," he told me. " And I am, by the way, extremely hun-gry. I trust that your taste in our lunch matches mine."

" I bespoke mutton chops preceded by a mulligatawny soup," I told him. " Mrs. Hudson told me that she had some excellent mutton delivered this morning."

" Excellent. If you will be kind enough to ring for her, I will tell you of my interview with brother Mycroft while we eat."

Mrs. Hudson brought the food in answer to my ringing the bell, and as he had promised, Sherlock Holmes pro-ceeded to acquaint me with the morning's events.

" As I had suspected would be the case, Mycroft was not in the best of moods when I told him that we had been unable to find the letter. I passed him the document that you discovered, and this went some way to improving his temper. He was totally unaware that such a document had even been considered, let alone the fact that it actually ex-isted, and it gave him pause for thought, I can tell you. By the by, I gave you full credit for its discovery, and the rec-ognition that it was of significance. Accordingly, Mycroft requested me to pass on his appreciation and his thanks to you."

" That is most gratifying to hear."

" However, the reminder of the fact that we failed to locate Mahoney after allowing him to leave Ledbury Hall put
him in such a passion as I have never before seen. Even
when we were children, he never treated me in this way
before. I find it intolerable to be in such a position. He
called Hopkins into the room. I will admit that Hopkins
is one of the more competent and efficient members of the
Force, but even so, he is not remotely in the same class as
myself as regards the science of detection and the study of
the criminal mind. Mycroft then proceeded to address me
in terms that one would not use to a servant, in front of
this mere policeman. It was an utter humiliation, Watson,
and it will be a long time before I can consider forgiving
Mycroft for his actions in this regard."

" And what now ? "

" I washed my hands of the whole affair, as graceful-
ly as I could manage without, I trust, seeming to appear
overly petty in front of Hopkins. Hopkins is, as I say,
one of our more intelligent police officers, and it may well
be that I will find myself working with him at some time
in the future. I trust that Mycroft's words have not poi-
soned the whole Metropolitan Police force against me. It
will, I repeat, be some considerable time before I am able
to forgive Mycroft his words and his attitude towards me,
though. In any case, I have put this whole Tosca business
behind me. The official word, which will be backed by
Hopkins in his capacity as a representative of the police,
is that Tosca suffered a stroke, and no suspicious circumstances pertain to his decease.

" I am, however, still extremely vexed regarding the
whole business. In the meantime, I feel my soul requires
some solace, which is not to be found here. Would you do
me the pleasure of accompanying me to the concert hall

this afternoon, where we may escape the turmoil of the city and lose ourselves in the immortal strains of the masters of the past ? "

I readily assented, as it was clear to my eyes that Holmes was under some severe emotional strain, as was occasionally the case, and required companionship, if not conversation. I feared that he might easily revert to some of his previous injurious habits were he to be left alone, and it was therefore with a sense of relief that I heard him offer this suggestion as to how he might spend his time. During the entire concert, he sat with his eyes closed, but it was clear from the movements of his hand in time with the music that he was not asleep. However, much of his tension appeared to have left him when we left the hall, and he even made one or two comments of a humorous nature.

On our journey home, we walked through the Park, with Holmes maintaining his amiable mood, and returned to Baker-street, where Mrs. Hudson handed an envelope to Holmes as we started to ascend the steps to the sitting-room. " This arrived about an hour ago," she informed him.

" Ha ! " Holmes exclaimed after we had entered the room and he had opened the envelope. " This is a pleasant surprise, I must confess ! "

His words caused me to start, occupied as I was with pouring two glasses of brandy and water. " What is this ? "

" It is from brother Mycroft. He has actually apologised to me for his words earlier today. This is a remarkable development. To anyone who knows my brother, this is almost as remarkable as if he were to suddenly sprout wings and fly. In all the years of my life, I think I have known him to offer an apology only once, and that was to my mother, under threat of severe punishment by my father. And he adds that he has also sent a message to Hopkins, explaining that his words to me were spoken in the heat of the moment, and are not to be regarded seriously. Well, well." He accepted the drink that I proffered, and regarded the paper once more. " He says that he now recognises that there was little that I could do to recover the letter or to detain Mahoney. He thanks me and you for locating the missive from the Pope, and that he now regards me as being free to return to Atherstoke and pursue my investigations along the lines that he has recommended to me. How generous of him, to be sure."

" Then there is peace between the Holmes brothers ? " I asked.

Holmes smiled thinly. " I think you may regard that as being the case. It seems that I can now wash my hands of the whole of this wretched affair, and return with a clear conscience to my previous business."

With those words, he believed that he had closed the book on this case. Although he made discreet enquiries at intervals to both his brother and to Hopkins regarding the progress of the case, the answer was always in the negative. It appeared that Mahoney and the letter had disappeared from the face of the earth, not to be seen again. Indeed, I had almost forgotten about the events until the advent of John Alderton as a client, and the events described below.

Part II – The Willows, Windsor

Mr. James Alderton

–

Baker-street, London

 T was some three or four months after this that the following incidents took place. At that time it was still necessary, for reasons connected with my practice, for me to live away from the lodgings in Baker-street which I had at times shared with Holmes. However, our friendship continued at the same warm level that it had always enjoyed, and my first port of call, accordingly, on my return to the metropolis was at the well-known door of 221B Baker-street, and the seventeen steps leading to the rooms that were so familiar to me.

On being admitted to the room, I beheld Holmes studying a sheet of paper which he held in one hand. With the other, he waved me nonchalantly towards my accustomed armchair before passing the paper over to me with a chuckle.

" What do you make of this ? " he asked me.

I took the proffered paper, and read aloud. "' Dear Mr Holmes, I have been informed that you extend your help to those faced with problems of an unusual nature. I therefore propose to call on you at half past three tomorrow afternoon in order to explain to you such a problem concerning our domestic servants, which I feel will be of interest to you. Yours sincerely, James Alderton.'"

" So now I am to advise the general public on the hiring and dismissal of kitchen maids and cooks, it would appear," Holmes laughed.

" It would certainly seem to be something in this line." I pulled out my watch. " It is now twenty-five minutes after the hour. Your client will be with you in five minutes. Perhaps I should go ? "

" No, no. As always, you are welcome to share whatever points of interest that this case may bring us, though I fear such will be sadly lacking here. I trust, by the way, that your trip to Bedfordshire was satisfactory ? "

" Indeed it was," I assured him, and was about to expound further when I was interrupted by the voice of Mrs Hudson announcing the arrival of James Alderton. When our visitor was admitted to the room, his eyes fell on me, but quickly passed to Sherlock Holmes, to whom he presented a card.

" Who is this ? " he asked in an abrupt tone. " I trust that my private affairs about which I consult you may be regarded as confidential ? "

" This is my colleague, friend, and occasional biographer, Dr Watson," Holmes introduced me. " Anything you say before me may also be safely said before him."

" In that case, I am content to take your word for it."

" But please, Mr Alderton, or perhaps I should address you as Major Alderton, do sit down and take this chair near the fire. I fear that our English climate must come as an unpleasant surprise to you after the heat of Burma."

Our visitor displayed some visible surprise at Holmes' words. " How in the world did you come to know my Army rank, and how did you guess that I have been in Burma ? "

" There was no guessing involved, sir. Immediately you entered the room, it was obvious to me that you had recently returned from the tropics. It was also clear that you have been a military man, and one used to command at a relatively senior level. Your age would preclude you from attaining a rank higher than that of Major, and an additional clue was provided in your letter to me where you started to put your former rank in brackets following your name, but thought better of it and crossed it out, though not sufficiently to prevent my deducing that this was indeed the level you had reached in your former career. From further examination, I would guess that you have been invalided out of the Army, though this is more Watson's department than my own."

" Yes, yes, indeed you are correct," answered our visitor. " I have recently retired from the army, as you say, on grounds of ill-health. I contracted malaria while serving in Rangoon, and the disease was of sufficient severity as to necessitate the resigning of my commission. But I am completely mystified as to how you had established that it was in Burma that I served, and not in some other part of the Empire ? "

Holmes chuckled. " As to that, my dear sir, it is

simplicity itself. You bear on your watch chain a small charm, which I recognise as being a likeness of the Buddha, whose teachings are followed in that part of the world. The workmanship is of a style familiar to me, that of the artisans of Southeast Asia, of Siam and that area. Since, to the best of my knowledge, the British Army does not maintain an establishment in Siam, I am forced to conclude that the trinket in question was purchased, or at least had its origin in Burma."

" Well, you make it seem remarkably simple," laughed our guest.

" Just so," commented Holmes, with a touch of asperity. " You mentioned in your letter that you had problems regarding your servants. I think I should tell you that domestic problems are not my primary field of interest."

" Even so, I think that you will find this to be a problem that merits some attention. Let me tell you of my story, and you may then decide for yourself whether it is a subject that warrants the expertise of Mr Sherlock Holmes."

" Well, well," Holmes smiled. " You certainly make it sound intriguing." Having requested and received permission to smoke, he leaned back in his chair, his eyes half closed, and his fingertips steepled together in that familiar pose that betokened his extreme attention to the matter at hand.

" You are absolutely correct in your description of my circumstances," began Alderton. " I served in the 32nd Regiment of Foot, rising to the rank of major, with my last posting in Burma. While I was in Burma, I became acquainted with, and fell in love with the daughter of one of my senior officers, and we were married with her father's wholehearted consent. He foresaw a bright future for me in the Army, and though I will not say that he was responsible for advancing my career, at any rate he did little to hinder it. As I say, I rose in my command, maybe a little faster than others who were contemporary with me, and my marriage was—indeed, still is—as happy as one can imagine. But as you no doubt know, from your experience of human nature, even the best of lives on a happy course may strike the rock of misfortune at times. And so it was with me.

" I had been dispatched, together with my company, to the south of the country. It was at that time, by the way, that I purchased the small charm that you remarked earlier. In that part of the world, particularly in the district to which my company had been sent, the land is wet and marshy, and the foul air emanating from the swamps brought low many of my men as well as myself. I appeared to be among those worst affected by the disease, and my malaria is still a torment to me at times. My dear Harriet nursed me on my return from the south, but I was so badly stricken by the malady that I was forced to quit the army and return to England with a small pension. I have been lucky enough to find work in the City, and I am not, whatever my other disadvantages may be, short of money. Harriet's father has also been remarkably generous to me in my misfortune, and I am happy to say that although I could not be described as wealthy, my financial situation is comfortable. I say this," he added hastily, " not in any spirit of pride or boasting, but to reassure you that I will be able to meet any financial demands that I may incur as a result of engaging your services.

" I arrived in England, accompanied by my wife, some two months ago, and rented a charming house in Windsor. Harriet felt, and I agreed with her, that residing in the city of London would not be beneficial to my health. On moving into the house, we immediately felt ourselves at home, and I confess that, despite my disappointment at having been forced to leave my chosen profession, it was a relief for me to feel the cool of the English climate after the sweltering heat of the tropics.

" Our needs are modest, and we employ a cook and a girl who performs the functions of a general servant. We live quietly, but have made the acquaintance of several of our neighbours, and we occasionally visit them, and they us. Imagine our surprise when, just under two weeks ago, a girl appeared on our doorstep asking about the position of kitchen maid in our household. My wife received her, informed her that there was no such position available, and sent her away. The next day, it was my turn to answer the door to another girl who was likewise enquiring after a similar position."

" Had your wife informed you of the previous applicant for this non-existent post ? " interrupted Holmes.

" No, I only learnt of this after I had informed her of my own experience. Naturally, when I first heard the girl's explanation, I assumed that she had come to the wrong house. I asked her which household she was seeking, assuming that she had mistaken our house for that of one of our neighbours, and proposed to redirect her to the correct location. To my astonishment, she gave my name and my address. On my explaining to her that we were not seeking her services, she burst into tears, and explained to me that she had spent a good deal of money to travel from London for the express purpose of seeking employment with us. My wife was absent, visiting friends, or I would have requested her to provide some comfort to the poor girl. As it was, it was almost impossible for me to get any sense out of her in her near hysterical condition. I felt that the least

I could do was to compensate her for her wasted journey, and I pressed the money into her hand before dismissing her.

" On my wife's return, I informed her of the incident, and she in turn informed me of the similar circumstance on the previous day. Neither of us could understand how such a coincidence could have come about, but we felt that this was the end of the matter. As it turned out, this was not the case. After two days, the incident repeated itself. On this occasion, we were both at home. At about half past five in the evening, when I had just returned from the City, our maid informed my wife that a girl at the door wished to speak with her.

" ' Come with me, John,' Harriet said to me. ' It may well be that it is another of those girls who believe that we wish to employ a kitchen maid.' It transpired that she was correct in this assumption. The girl informed us that she had been dispatched by an agency who had been requested to provide a kitchen maid for our household. Once again, she had our address and our name correctly. Indeed, she had it written on a piece of paper that she carried with her. I requested the name of the agency who had dispatched her, and she informed me that it was the firm of Edwards & Lowe of Upper Holland Street."

" The name is not familiar to me," murmured Holmes, and turning to me. " Be so good as to make a note of that name, Watson," he instructed me. " Pray continue."

" Once again, on hearing that there was no post available, the girl appeared to become hysterical. As on the previous occasion, I provided her with the money she claimed to have spent on her travel from London. However, I now had the name of an agency, and the possible source of this annoyance. I therefore determined to pay a visit to the offices of this agency the next day in order to rectify the situation.

" Accordingly, during my lunch hour on the following day, I made my way to Upper Holland Street in search of Edwards & Lowe. Unfortunately, I did not have sufficient time to locate the agency on that day, nor the next, since the girl had been unable to provide us with the number of the house in the street. At length, I discovered the office, which appeared to consist of a single room on the second floor of number 57, but it was closed during the lunch hour, and when I made a point of revisiting it after work, it was likewise closed. I therefore wrote a message on a page torn from my memorandum book, addressed it to whom it might concern, and slipped it into the letter-box in the office door, requesting them to make contact with me. This was one week ago, and since then I have heard nothing."

" I take it that you have visited the office since delivering your message ? "

" I have indeed, on three separate occasions, each at a different time of the day. On every visit, I have left a message, similar to the first."

" And have any more girls presented themselves as applicants for this non-existent post ? "

" Indeed they have, several times. The last such was last night. I am sorry to report on the most recent occasion that I became quite incensed and turned the applicant away from the door weeping. Also, regarding the past three girls who have appeared at our door, I have instructed them specifically to pass on my message to the agency of Edwards & Lowe, instructing them to cease this harassment, but it would appear that my appeals have had no effect."

" So you would wish me to seek out this agency, and

demand on your behalf that they desist ? "

" That is precisely what I wish you to do, Mr. Holmes."

" Have you informed the police of this ? " I asked him.

He turned to me. " I have informed the local constabulary of these events, but they claim that they are unable to proceed with the matter, since no crime appears to have been committed. It was they who recommended that I seek out a private detective, and since your name appears at the head of any list of those practicing the profession, I decided to seek your services."

" Very well. Tell me, have you experienced any other strange incidents ? Any more unexpected visitors ? "

" It is strange that you should ask that question of me. When we first took possession of the house, a positive stream of tramps visited the back door demanding food. I strongly disapprove of encouraging such people, and I instructed the cook and the girl to turn them away without meeting their requests. On occasion, I was in the house when they called, and I personally saw them off the premises, brandishing my revolver—unloaded, naturally, but they were not to know this."

" When did these unwanted visits commence, and for how long did they continue ? "

" They started about three days after we moved into the house, and lasted for about a week. Perhaps three or four of these tramps called every day during that period."

" That is indeed a remarkable number," said Holmes. " Of course, you may not be aware of the secret chalk signs that these 'gentlemen of the road' use to indicate that a household is generous in its offerings to them."

" I have heard of such," replied our visitor, " and I took the trouble to scrutinise the area around our house—the gate and such—for any markings of this kind, but was unable to see any that would provide information to our unwelcome visitors."

" It is possible," mused Holmes, " that the previous occupant of the house was generous in his largesse to these mendicants. You say that you are renting this property ? "

" That is correct."

" Do you know anything of the previous tenant ? "

" I believe, from our neighbours, that he was a quiet man, unmarried, who kept himself to himself and was rarely seen in public. Indeed, now that I come to recall it, even his name would appear to be unknown to me."

" That can easily be obtained. The name and address of the agents through whom you are renting the house ? " Alderton told him, and I added the name to the notes I had been continuing to record. " I will pay a visit to them and make enquiries. It may well have some relevance."

" If you can clear up this matter, it will be a great relief to my wife. She is almost at her wits' end, I can tell you, and the matter has been preying on my mind as well, of course. What with the tramps, this succession of applicants for a position that does not exist, and the problems with the drains, she has told me that we will have to leave the house by the end of the month."

" The drains ? " asked Holmes.

" Yes, indeed. We noticed a stench of decay which appeared to emanate from the region of the drains about a week after we took possession of the house. Naturally, we informed the agents, and they dispatched workmen to examine the building and the foundations, but they could discover nothing untoward. If anything, the smell has become worse over the past few weeks, and on a hotter day, it is almost intolerable."

" Dear me, it would seem that you have truly been

unlucky in your choice of dwelling," answered Holmes. " I will investigate on your behalf and attempt to discover if there is any information from this agency or from the letting agent that will help to shed light on your mysteries."

" I am truly grateful to you," Alderton said, rising to his feet. " The mere fact that I have engaged your services in this regard will help to put Harriet's mind at rest, as it has already done mine."

" I will inform you as soon as I learn anything of relevance," Holmes assured him, as he showed him to the door and ushered him out of the house.

" Well, Watson, what do you make of all this ? " he asked me as he returned to the room, rubbing his hands together. " It has all the makings of a nice little mystery, does it not ? "

" You feel that there is some vengeful motive here ? This constant dispatching of tramps and servant girls is intended to repay some kind of injury or slight, either originally committed by Alderton himself, or by his wife ? "

" That would certainly seem to fit the facts as we know them at present. However, we should bear in mind that he is recently returned from abroad. Unless the injury was perpetrated before he went overseas, it is hard to know what he could have done in such a short space of time to provoke such hostility."

" The wife ? " I suggested.

" Meaning that these acts may be directed against the wife rather than the husband ? Again, though, we know nothing of the past history in this case. We need data, Watson, data."

" I was thinking rather in terms of a jealous ex-suitor."

" Always seeking the romantic explanation, eh ? That is indeed a possibility. The worm of revenge in these cases may gnaw away for many years, it is true. I think we must take ourselves to Upper Holland Street, and discover who it was who placed these demands for unwanted servant girls. Come, there is no time like the present. It is a fine afternoon, and the walk will invigorate us." He snatched up his hat and stick, and I followed him.

At the address in Upper Holland Street that Alderton had provided, we made our way up several flights of dingy badly lit stairs to the second floor, where we came to the door with the name of Edwards & Lowe inscribed on a cardboard square rudely tacked to the door. Although it was early evening, the hour was still such that one could confidently expect an office to be occupied, but on knocking at the door, we received no answer. Turning the handle established the fact that the door was locked.

" This was to be expected," remarked Holmes, bringing out his set of picklocks. " Pray keep watch. It would be inconvenient for us to spend the night in the cells as suspected burglars." In the event, it was a matter of less than a minute before the door silently swung open. We entered, and closed the door behind us. The room was sparsely furnished in the manner typical of such offices—a crude desk with a typewriter on it, and a few chairs, together with a cabinet which was presumably used for storing papers. It was to that last that Sherlock Holmes strode, and pulled open the unlocked drawer to remove a few sheets of paper, which he spread out on the desk.

" This is Alderton's address," he said, pointing to the first sheet. " And these are receipts from newspapers for the placement of advertisements. Make a note of the newspapers and the dates, while I continue the search. These are blank sheets of paper," rolling one into the typewriter and producing a few lines using the machine before pocketing the paper. He opened the other drawer of the cabinet, and those of the desk, but failed to discover anything else which would lead to the identity of the occupants of the room. There was a door behind the desk which presumably led to the next room, but on our attempting to open it, we discovered it was locked.

" It is obvious that the room has been used in the recent past. Alderton informed us that he had posted his messages through the letterbox in the door, did he not ? There is nothing in the cage attached to the inside of the door designed to catch such messages. This argues that on at least one occasion in the last week, someone has entered and removed the messages."

" And we may assume that this office was used to interview the girls, and then to dispatch them to Alderton," I added.

" I am certain of that. You have a list of the newspapers and dates ? Excellent. We will call on them tomorrow, since it is late now. Let us go." He replaced the papers in the cabinet, and I was about to open the door into the corridor, when Holmes stopped me. " Wait." His keen ears had obviously heard the sound of another door opening, for in a few seconds I could distinguish the sound of a door being closed and locked, followed by the sound of footsteps making their way towards the stairs. " Now," he told me, and we darted out of the room. " I must re-lock the door. Keep watch again," he ordered, and I did so.

After he had locked the door, we made our way down the stairs to the street, and as we passed through the front door of the building, our paths crossed with that of a seedy-looking man in an overcoat that had seen better days, as had the bowler hat perched on the back of his head.

Holmes took my arm and marched us away from the

door before he hissed in my ear, " I would lay money that man is either Edwards or Lowe and will be going to the office we have just vacated. Return to Baker-street and wait for me there. I wish to see where this leads."

I therefore returned to the lodgings as instructed, but in the event I was forced to wait for a relatively little time before Holmes re-joined me there. He was smiling ruefully as he threw his hat into a corner.

" Never underestimate the native cunning of your Irishman," he told me, lighting his pipe.

" Why ? What happened ? "

" I slipped in after the gentleman whom we saw enter the building as we were leaving, and followed him up the stairs. As we surmised, he was indeed connected with the agency whose room we visited. He entered, and the gaslight in the room was lit. I waited, supposing myself to be unobserved, at the end of the passageway, waiting for him to emerge. The light in the room went off, but no-one emerged from the room. Eventually, I discovered that my bird had flown."

" How do you mean ? "

" Do you recall the locked door behind the desk ? After waiting for about ten minutes following the extinguishing of the light, I went cautiously to the room—there might well have been a trap laid for me, after all. This time, the door from the passageway was unlocked, and I let myself in. I confess that I was half-expecting to be attacked, but I had my weighted stick with me, and I was prepared for such an eventuality. It was plain to me, though, as soon as I struck a match, that the door behind the desk had been opened, and I followed the path that my quarry had obviously taken.

" Once in the next room, all became clear. This room

had two additional doors, one leading onto the same passageway as the one from which I had just come, and the other leading to another one leading from the first at right angles, and invisible from where I had been standing. This passage led to a flight of stairs, which was obviously the route which our friend had taken.

" My vanity is hurt, I confess. I pride myself on my ability to follow another man without his being aware of it, but in this instance, I failed. Possibly I dropped some small object or made some other noise while I was moving up the stairs behind him."

" But you mentioned that he was Irish. How did you come to that conclusion ? "

" That was simplicity itself. On the desk of the empty office lay a packet which had once contained cigarettes of a brand favoured almost exclusively by Irishmen. To add to this belief, the name of Hannigan, a common Irish name, together with the number 23, had been rudely scrawled on the packet."

" The meaning of that ? "

Holmes shrugged. " Who can say ? Quite possibly a house number or some such. Without the name of the street, naturally it is useless to us. We must therefore follow our original plan and visit the newspaper offices tomorrow."

Mrs. Harriet Alderton

–

Windsor

OUR round of the newspaper offices brought us a little closer to discovering the identity of the mystery surrounding the agency of Edwards & Lowe. Each of the five newspapers that we visited had printed the advertisement once only. In each case, the advertisement had been placed personally, seemingly by the Irishman who had been Holmes' quarry on the previous evening, and had been paid for in cash. The name given on the receipts at the different newspapers varied, but was always a name that is associated with the Emerald Isle. On one point, all our informants were agreed; that he was possessed of a strong Irish accent.

The wording of the advertisement placed in the different newspapers was identical in each case, stating that a vacancy existed for a kitchen maid to live and work in the Windsor area. The wages offered in the advertisement were good ones, and it was plain that such an advertisement would attract a large number of applicants. The address at which prospective servants were to present themselves was that which we had visited, and the name of the agency was plainly stated as that of Edwards & Lowe. One notable feature of the advertisement was that the time at which applicants were to visit the office was limited to between ten in the morning and half past the hour. Outside those times, it was clearly stated that no applications would be entertained.

" That time of day being, no doubt, when Alderton would be assumed to be at work in the City, and therefore would be the most unlikely time for him to make enquiries," remarked Holmes as we made our way from the fourth to the fifth newspaper office.

" We seem to have accomplished little," I grumbled.

" By no means," Holmes contradicted me. " For example, we now know the appearance of one of the main players in this game. I should certainly know him again were I to meet him. We have established that he is an Irishman, and that another of his confederates is probably called Hannigan. That last is not an established fact, of course, but I think we may regard it as being probable. We also know that he is taking great care to hide his identity, and he is obviously very much aware of his surroundings—in particular of those following him. Indeed, in his way, we may regard him as a professional in his chosen field."

" What field would that be ? " I asked curiously.

" He has all the marks of an anarchist or a

Fenian. Naturally, we cannot confirm this until we have the pleasure of meeting him face to face, but it strikes me as being a very real possibility."

" But what in the world can he want with Alderton ? "

" There, my dear Watson, I confess to being baffled. We must make our way to Windsor this evening, and report our findings to Alderton while attempting to discover this connection between him or his wife and this unknown son of Erin. But before we do that, I suggest that we make our way to the letting agent to determine whether there is anything to be learned regarding the previous tenant."

The letting agent, a Mr. Fanshawe, was suspicious of our motives at first, but when Holmes identified himself and explained that he was working for the current tenant of The Willows, for that transpired to be the name of the house currently occupied by Alderton and his wife, he became extremely cooperative.

" I remember the previous tenant quite well," he told us, " since I attended to his business myself. He took the house some six months ago, so he was only living there for four months or less."

" Can you tell us a little more about him ? "

" He appeared to be some kind of foreigner from the way he was dressed, though he spoke English perfectly well. I had guessed that he had lived overseas for some time, as his skin was considerably darker than yours or mine. He told me that he had recently returned from the colonies, which explained his colouring. A small man, I would have to say, shorter than either of you two gentlemen. He was on the far side of fifty years old, I would say, with hair that was turning white."

" Can you give us his name ? "

" His surname was Campion, but I would have to search

my books to discover his Christian name. If you will wait one moment, please, I can discover it for you." He leafed through a ledger. " Ah yes, Edmund."

" Indeed," remarked Holmes, smiling. " Watson, there is no need for you to write down the name. It is already familiar to me." A little offended by this brusque rejection of my assistance, I closed my notebook.

" How long ago did he leave the house ? "

" Do you know, I believe I am unable to provide you with that information. I do not mean that I am unwilling to do so," he added quickly, observing the expression on Holmes' face, " but that I am unable to do so. The notice terminating the lease arrived by post. I have it here." He extracted a sheet of paper from the ledger and passed it to Holmes.

" I see that it has been written on a typewriter," remarked my friend. " But signed personally, I see. The signature matches that on the lease ? "

" You may see for yourself," the agent invited him, passing over another sheet of paper.

Holmes made no comment, but examined the two documents in silence, his brow furrowed, and examining them under his lens, before passing them back to the agent with a word of thanks.

We left the agent's after a few more minutes of conversation between Holmes and Fanshawe, and I turned to my friend. " That man described just now was Monsignor Mahoney whom we pursued from Ledbury Hall after the murder of Cardinal Tosca, was it not ? No doubt you did not wish me to write down his alias as you already were aware of his real name. What, however, if he were still using that name ? Would it not be easier to discover him if this were also added to the description used by those searching for him ? "

Holmes laughed. " I fear, Watson, that your Protestant upbringing has left you strangely ignorant of certain matters. At the school that Mycroft and I attended, it was naturally well known that Edmund Campion was the name of an English martyr of the old faith who was hideously executed in the sixteenth century."

I was curious. Holmes had been reticent in his mentions of such matters of faith to me in the past, and I had no knowledge of the way in which he, let alone Mycroft, had been educated. It was now clear to me how Mycroft had been able to retain such good relations with the Holy See, and possibly why Holmes could find himself involved in certain cases somewhat against his will. However, I determined to hold my peace on the subject, knowing that he was more often than not reluctant to speak of these things in any detail.

" But," Holmes continued, before I was able to say anything in reply, " I am sure we find ourselves on a familiar trail once more. You are undoubtedly correct in making that connection. The date we have just been given for the start of his lease of the property corresponds to the date when he left Ledbury Hall."

" Do you think there is some connection between Mahoney and these mysterious visits by the tramps and by the servants ? "

" It would seem to me to be more than likely that there is such a link," replied Holmes, " but at present I am unable to tell you of its nature."

" The date that he quit the house and cancelled the lease arrangement is a matter of a mere week or even less before Alderton moved in there to take up the lease," I remarked. " Does that not seem somewhat strange to you ? "

" It may well be strange," he agreed. " On the other hand, I am reluctant to attach too many threads at
this stage in the proceedings. We need data if we are to
disentangle this case—or should I say, these cases, for
although we seem to have established a connection, we cannot be sure of the link between them, or even if such a link
exists. To Windsor, therefore."

The town of Windsor is well enough known for it to
need no introduction from me. Willow Grove proved to be
a pleasantly set older building quite close to the Castle,
living up to Alderton's description of it as " charming",
and the door was opened by a servant, presumably the par-
lour-maid about whom Alderton had informed us. We
sent in our cards, enquiring whether Mrs. Alderton was
at home.

While we were waiting, Holmes bent down to murmur
in my ear. " For a retired major, presumably on half pay,
Alderton seems to be doing himself rather well, would you
not say ? "

I was forced to agree. The house was well furnished with
a number of Oriental knick-knacks, which obviously had
not formed part of the original appointments of the house,
and were quite clearly of some value. A large bronze statue representing some aspect of the Buddhist faith stood
guardian at one end of the hall, fixing us with its inscruta-
ble gaze.

" He did inform us that he was not in financial straits,"
I reminded Holmes. " Even though many of these objects are obtainable in their home country for considerably
less than one would pay here, I would judge some of these
to fetch a tidy sum were they to be offered for sale. This
bronze, for example," and I pointed to a small statue of
some many-limbed deity, " would be a prize in some

collections, I believe. Though I myself lacked the means to collect such *objets* during my time in India, some of the senior officers in my regiment could avail themselves of the opportunity, and some had collections that would not disgrace a small museum. It was from them that I learned a little of the styles and subjects portrayed."

" You have hidden depths, Watson," Holmes smiled.

At this moment, the maid returned, and informed us that Mrs. Alderton was at home and would receive us. We were shown into the drawing-room, where a young woman sat sewing. Despite the warmth of the summer afternoon, she was wearing a thick dress, with a shawl covering her shoulders, a mode of dress which I would have considered more suitable for the winter than for the present time of year.

" No, do not rise, I beg you," Sherlock Holmes said to her, taking her hand. " This is Doctor Watson," indicating me, " and I am Sherlock Holmes. Your husband has probably informed you that I have been retained to assist with the mystery of the unwanted maids who have come seeking employment at your door."

She smiled. " Yes, James told me that he had secured your services. He should return soon, and you may tell him all that you have discovered."

" In the meantime, Mrs. Alderton, I would greatly appreciate your account of the recent events."

" I am sure James told you everything."

" Even so, there are times when a woman's eye will catch details that may be overlooked by us mere male members of the species."

Holmes' flattery appeared to work, and Mrs. Alderton smiled at us in reply. " That is true, I suppose. I may tell you at the outset that I am sorry that we ever came to this miserable house. Oh, it may appear to be a pleasant enough dwelling, and I suppose that in its way it matches that appearance, but I can tell you, Mr. Holmes, that it has not been a happy home for James and me. James mentioned the tramps to you ? "

" He did indeed."

" Almost from the first day we were here these horrible dirty men made their appearance at the back door, begging and asking for food. I am not a hard-hearted woman, Mr. Holmes—James is all for sending them packing without any charity—but I always feel it is my duty to assist those less fortunate than myself."

I could not prevent myself from interjecting. " A very worthy attitude," I said to her.

She turned and smiled at me. " Thank you, Dr. Watson. However, the tramps that presented themselves at our back door were of a type that I do not wish to encounter. There are some—I do not know if you are well acquainted with the type, Mr. Holmes—who appear to have fallen from a higher station in life than the one they occupy at present. In such cases, one cannot help but feel that some charity is due them. These, though, were uniformly scoundrels of the lowest class. With some mendicants of the better type such as I have just described to you, I have no hesitation in allowing them to enter the kitchen and to eat their food under the eyes of the cook—"

" Has the cook been with you long ? " Holmes asked, interrupting her.

" No, Mrs. Wiles has only been with us since we moved into the house. I will not quite say that she came as part of the furniture of the house," she smiled, " but she had worked for the previous tenant, and wished to continue working in the house."

" Indeed. And does she sleep on the premises ? "

" No, she lives locally, and goes home of an evening after dinner. The girl Lucy who admitted you sleeps here. Other than James and myself, she is the only one occupying this house after eight in the evening. In any case... What was I saying ? "

" You were telling us of the tramps who visited the house," I reminded her.

" Oh yes, so I was. The kind of tramp who visited us, as I say, was uniformly, without exception, a foul slovenly brute, and I could never dream of allowing such a person into the house."

" You spoke to them yourself, I believe ? " asked Holmes.

" I spoke to some of them. Mrs. Wiles begged me to do so on more than one occasion."

" Was there anything that you observed in common about these men, other than the dirt and general ragged appearance ? " Holmes enquired of her.

" There was indeed, now that you come to mention it," she answered him. " I believe they all spoke with an Irish accent."

" Maybe not unusual," I remarked, " if they had all been labourers working on the same task, which had ceased, and cast them all onto the road together."

" Maybe," said Holmes, though the tone of his voice told me that he was not convinced by my supposition. " You are certain of that, Mrs. Alderton ? "

" I cannot be completely certain, no, but I can be reasonably sure of it. When I refused them their demands, I expected anger and threats, I confess, and I had steeled myself for such antagonism, but it never came."

" You are a brave woman," Holmes said to her.

" I am a soldier's daughter, and I have faced down

rebellious natives in my time," she said, with a touch of steel in her voice. " I am not about to shrink from confronting a drunken wretch." There was a touch of fire in her eyes as she uttered these words, and I confess that I, even though happily married, felt a touch of envy towards Alderton with regard to his marriage to this fine woman. " James, on the other hand..." She shook her head. " He would have no business with these men, and he chased two of them away with his revolver one day. After that, they never returned."

" And you have had problems with the drains, I believe ? "

She sighed. " The stench has nearly driven us out of the house on some days. Having lived in the East, I had imagined myself to be immune to such things, but it has been truly appalling, especially on hot days. James is in the City on weekdays during the day, so he has escaped the worst."

" I confess I smell nothing except the pot pourri here in this room," said Holmes.

" Today is not the worst of days and, as you say, the pot pourri masks many smells. Do you wish to experience the foul odour for yourself ? I will gladly get Lucy to conduct you to the spot in the house where you may take your fill of it."

" Later, I will certainly wish to do that. And the servants ? Or rather, the girls who wish to be servants ? "

She sighed again. " This was not perhaps as frightening as the visits of the mendicants, but it was distressing, all the same. We seemed to have a regular procession of these girls coming to the door, convinced that we were seeking a kitchen-maid."

" While in fact, you keep only the two servants, the girl

Lucy and the cook Mrs. Wiles, and have no wish to employ more ? I am correct in that ? "

" That is how matters stand at the moment. It may well be that our circumstances will improve and we will require the services of a kitchen-maid at some time in the future, but that time, I fear, is a little way off."

" It must seem a little hard for you after your life in the East," remarked Holmes sympathetically.

She smiled faintly. " I suppose that it may be regarded as such, but it is not all a bed of roses there. It is true that we had many servants in Burma, but believe me, it can be more trouble than it is worth to maintain such a household. I confess to feeling the cold, though, even on a day such as this, which is considered a temperate one in this country. I fear I will fall victim to rheumatism or some such malady."

" I have heard it said that such is the case at times," Holmes told her gravely. " But to return to the girls. Was there any feature common to all of them that you noticed, as you did with the tramps ? They possessed no accent or manner of speech in common, for example ? "

Mrs. Alderton frowned slightly as she appeared to recall the matter. " No, there is nothing of that kind that I can remember. They all seemed to be of the type that would apply for such a post, should it exist."

" And they were all sent by this agency which goes by the name of Edwards & Lowe ? "

" So it would seem. Some of the girls were almost hysterical when they were informed there was no post available, and it was difficult for me to make sense of their words."

" And there was no mistake on their part regarding the address to which they had been dispatched ? "

" None whatsoever. All had our name and our address, correctly written on a piece of paper."

" Do you have any of these pieces of paper ? "

" I believe James kept one or two to take to the agency when he visited their offices. It is possible that one is in the bureau now. If I may... ? " She rose and moved towards the article of furniture in question.

" Please do so."

After about a minute, she presented a small square of paper to Sherlock Holmes, who examined it closely. " May I keep this ? " he asked, and on receiving an answer in the affirmative, placed the paper carefully in his pocket-book. " Do you happen to know if your husband retained any others ? "

" You may ask him when he returns. I do not know." Our hostess sat, her hands folded demurely in her lap, as Holmes scribbled a note on his shirt-cuff.

" Have there been any other untoward incidents ? Any other strange visitors ? "

Mrs Alderton frowned. " Now that I come to recall the matter, I can think of one more. He was an Italian, or a Spaniard, or from some country such as that, by the look of him. I cannot be sure. His English was very good, though he spoke with a slight accent. He wanted to know who was living here, and on learning of our having taken the house, asked if I knew the whereabouts of the previous tenant. Of course, I was unable to answer his questions. The incident had completely slipped my mind until now, though. I do not think I even mentioned it to my husband."

Holmes considered this statement. " I have to ask you, Mrs. Alderton, whether you or your husband might have any enemies who could have instigated this harassment of your household ? "

" We have recently returned from Burma, and I feel it is most unlikely that James could have acquired any enemies in such a short space of time. As for myself, I was born in India, and this is the first time that I have been in England." She smiled. " As I mentioned earlier, I am still unused to the climate, which I find uncomfortably cold and very much not to my taste."

" But did your husband have no enemies in Burma ? "

" Other than some natives whom he was forced to bring to justice, and who felt that they had been treated unfairly by him, I do not think so. Of course, there were professional rivals in the Mess. The Army can be a highly competitive society—"

" I know well what you mean there," I broke in. " I witnessed this for myself in my time in India."

" Then you are aware of the rivalry. However, James has now retired from the service, and he is no longer in a position where he could be considered a threat to a brother officer's career."

" Is it possible that he could have offended a contemporary, or perhaps some other, who continues to bear him a grudge ? " asked Holmes.

" You would have to ask him that yourself," answered Mrs. Alderton. " I am not aware of any such incident or grudge."

" And you are similarly unaware of any such enmity that may have sprung up since his return to England ? "

" None whatsoever exists, as far as I am aware. James is working at Hollister & Co., as their manager in charge of trade with Burma. His knowledge of the country and of the language gained him that position, and I have it on the authority of my father that he was not given the post at another's expense."

" Did your father help your husband gain his current position ? "

" He did. He is on the board of directors, and when James found himself unable to continue his career in the army, my father contacted the firm, and ensured that James and I would have an income."

" Thank you, Mrs. Alderton. This has all been most helpful. Now if you could have me led to the source of the smell that has been disturbing you ? "

Mrs. Alderton pulled on the bell-rope. " Of course. You will forgive me if I do not accompany you, I trust ? "

" Naturally I do not expect you to disturb yourself."

The maid entered, summoned by the bell, and Mrs. Alderton ordered her to take us to the area where the smell was strongest. As she led us down the passageway, my nostrils were assailed by a foul odour. At first, this was almost unnoticeable, but as we neared the back of the house, the smell became stronger, until I found myself gagging on the stench, and was forced almost double with the violence of my coughing. Holmes, too, though seemingly less affected than I by the miasma, nevertheless turned to me with a look of disgust on his face.

" And this has been going on for how long ? " asked Holmes.

" Since the master and mistress moved in, sir. We noticed it a few days after."

" This is the worst place ? Where the smell is strongest ? " Holmes indicated the area where we were standing, which was a passageway leading to a small conservatory.

" Yes, sir, just here and the conservatory. It doesn't seem too bad in the kitchen, or the room over the kitchen, which is where I sleep. If it was like this, I have to tell you, sir, that I would have given in my notice long since."

" And who could blame you for doing so, if it were as bad as this ? Dear me, this really is terrible. And the workmen found nothing ? "

" No, sir. The men from the sanitary came round and they took up the floor, where the drains run under. They thought perhaps one of the pipes might have cracked or something, but it wasn't anything like that." By now we had entered the conservatory, and the smell, if anything, was worse.

" I see. If I may ? " Sherlock Holmes stooped, and examined the floor. " This is where they dug, then ? "

" No, sir. Not there. The drains are along the passageway, not in here."

" But the drains run under here ? "

" I couldn't rightly tell you, sir. The men from the sanitary didn't seem to think so, anyway. If you don't mind, I would sooner we left this place. The smell is something awful for me."

" By all means," I agreed hastily. " Come, Holmes, there is little to see here."

" That may be the case at present," he answered me. " Very well, let us be away. Lucy, please lead us back to your mistress."

When we had returned to the drawing-room, Holmes addressed Mrs. Alderton once more. " I agree with you that it is a most iniquitous smell, and I am sorry that the sanitary workers could not locate the cause."

" I am only thankful that it appears to be confined to a part of the house which we have little intention of using, and also for the fact that it does not appear to inconvenience Mrs. Wiles. We are lucky to have her, apparently. The standard of cooks in this country, according to those of our neighbours with whom I have spoken, is of an almost uniformly low standard."

" There is much truth in that," I agreed heartily.

" In any event," said Holmes, " with your permission, I would like to question Mrs. Wiles. She may be able to tell us of some points of interest concerning the house, since she has worked here in the past."

" Of course you may. James should be home in about twenty minutes. Will that provide you with enough time for your conversation ? "

" Admirably," answered Holmes. " No, no, do not rise. I am certain I can find my own way to the kitchen. Watson, come with me, if you would."

MRS. WILES

—

WINDSOR

 FOLLOWED Holmes as he led the way unerring-
ly to the kitchen of the house, where the cook
was busy preparing the dinner. She appeared as
a typical example of the profession, amply pro-
portioned, wearing a clean starched white apron.

" Yes ? " she said, somewhat crossly. " What can I do
for you two gentlemen ? "

" My name is Sherlock Holmes, and I would like to
speak with you when you have finished preparing the pastry for what promises to be, from the look of it, one of the
most delicious apple pies I have ever seen in my life."

" Ha ! You're a right charmer, you are, aren't you, sir ?

You can talk to me while I'm rolling out the pastry. I can still manage to do more than one thing at once, you know."

" Excellent. You worked in this house before Mr. And Mrs. Alderton came to live here, I believe ? "

" That's right. I did."

" For Mr. Campion ? "

" Who's that, sir ? Never heard of him."

" The previous tenant of this house."

" He wasn't called Campion, sir, I can tell you that. His name was Garnet. I think he was Thomas Garnet, if I remember the name on the envelopes addressed to him. Yes, Thomas Garnet was his name." She took the pastry from the bowl and started to roll it out on the marble slab.

" Was it indeed ? And he was tall, and rather pale-skinned, with ginger hair."

" Oh no, sir, I think you've got the wrong party completely there, sir. Mr. Garnet was a little man, not so tall as me, and he had brown skin from living in foreign parts, I heard. And his hair was nearly white, but you could tell that it had been dark at one time."

" Well, I do seem to be knocking at the wrong door, then," laughed Holmes. " Maybe you can tell me something about the Aldertons. Are they easy to please ? As easy as Mr. Garnet, for example ? "

" Well, as for Mr. Garnet, he'd eat anything I put in front of him with no questions asked, except on Fridays. He'd give me my money for the week's food every Monday and tell me to make it last until the Sunday. And he gave me enough that it didn't take a lot of doing on my part to make that happen. He always gave me enough. Take the Aldertons, though. They pay well and they're good enough people, but things have to be just right for madam. He's fine, though."

" So why did Mr. Garnet leave ? Why didn't you go with him if he was such a good employer ? "

She put down the rolling pin and looked Holmes in the eye. " Because he just walked out of the place without warning, that's why. I came in one morning and there was a note on the kitchen table telling me that he was not going to be living here any more. He left me two weeks' wages with the note, so I can't grumble about that side of things. But it was a bit of a shock, I can tell you."

" I can imagine that it was. Do you still have the note that he left you ? "

" Lord bless you, no sir. I used it to light the fire with that morning." She took the sheet of pastry and started to arrange it over the apples in the pie dish.

" But you recognised his writing ? "

She paused in her preparation of the pie. " Now that's a funny thing, sir. It wasn't in his writing. I'd seen his writing often enough. He used to leave me little messages like 'No meat today'. He wouldn't eat meat on a Friday, you see, like some of them won't, like I said to you just now. And he always used to write those to me. But this note telling me that he'd gone away was typed out on one of those machines."

" That is most suggestive," commented Holmes. " You mentioned that he would not eat meat on Fridays. Were there any other strange habits of his ? "

She put her hands on her hips as she considered the question. " Well, now you ask me, sir, I don't think he ever went outside. At least, not in the daylight. I am fairly sure that he went out at night, though, because I found some empty bottles which I had never seen before, and he must have bought them from the Dragon down the road."

" What sort of bottles, may I ask ? "

" Some sort of whiskey. Irish whiskey, I believe. And there were often some glasses there that had been drunk out of, which means he must have had company, though I never saw any such in the daytime."

" How very interesting. So Mr. Garnet had visitors in the evening ? Another question, if I may ? "

" Time is pressing, sir."

" I know that, but please, if I may. Was this house let furnished to the Aldertons ? "

" Yes it was. All the little Eastern knick-knack things came with the Aldertons, though. Now if you will excuse me, sir, I must be getting on."

" One last question, if you please. There is a smell in this house, as you know. Was this smell present when Mr. Garnet lived here ? "

" I never noticed it, sir. Not that I go to that part of the house much anyway. But Mr. Garnet used to like to go there and take his cup of tea and sit in the conservatory drinking it. I am sure he would have said something to me if he had smelled anything." She turned to her cooking with a determined air.

" Thank you, Mrs. Wiles, you have been most helpful. We will leave you to your pie. I regret that we will not be here this evening to partake of it." So saying, he left a half-crown unobtrusively on the corner of the table, an action that did not pass unnoticed.

" Why, thank you, sir," she said to us as we left the kitchen.

" I fancied that I heard Alderton return while we were conversing with the cook," Holmes said to me. " Let us return to the drawing-room. By the way, let me enlighten you as to the origin of Garnet's name."

" Another Catholic martyr of the Tudor years ? " I

hazarded.

" Precisely so. It would seem that Mahoney wished to send out signals to those who could read his code, so to speak, while at the same time maintaining his anonymity. A strange combination, to be sure."

As my friend had deduced, we discovered on reaching the drawing-room that Alderton had indeed returned, and he eagerly asked for news of the firm of Edwards & Lowe. Holmes informed him of the previous day's events, to which Alderton responded.

" What is their motive in persecuting us in this way ? " asked Mrs. Alderton.

" I think it is probably more accurate to say that they are not persecuting you at all. I will wager there is nothing in this business that concerns either of you personally. But a question, if I may ? "

" Of course."

" You took this house furnished, I believe ? "

" We did," agreed Alderton.

" There were no traces of the previous occupant ? Clothes ? Bed-linen and the like ? "

" Nothing along those lines when we viewed the property with the agent, certainly."

" Did you at any time find a typewriter among the effects here ? "

" A typewriter ? What a strange question. No, I have never seen anything of the sort here."

" Thank you. As I said just now, I do not believe that all these problems are concerned with you and Mrs. Alderton personally. They seem to me to be connected with the house—or to be precise about it, the recent history of the house."

" Then what is going on ? " demanded Alderton. " What

is the meaning of the foul smell ? "

" That seems to be a very bad business indeed," Holmes told him, shaking his head.

" What is going on here ? " Alderton repeated. " What is all this about ? "

" I have my suspicions," responded Holmes. " These are deep waters, and quite frankly, I fear for your safety. I saw just now that Mrs. Wiles appears to be preparing an excellent dinner for you. While you are eating it, I propose to contact London, and arrange for you and the girl to be moved to a place of safety which will be provided by the Government."

Mrs. Alderton's hands flew to her face, and she gasped. " Can we not take care of this problem ourselves ? James is an experienced soldier, after all, and he still has his revolver."

Holmes bowed to her. " Madam, with all due respect for you and for your husband's experience and courage, which I do not doubt for an instant, I hear that the men we find ourselves up against are desperate men who will stop at nothing to achieve their ends. I really must insist that you follow my instructions. I will go now and send telegrams to those responsible. Watson, you must stay here and help defend the place should it come to that pass, which I doubt." So saying, he strode to the door and left us.

" What in the world does he mean by all this ? Is he mad ? " asked Alderton of me.

" Sherlock Holmes is by no means mad," I answered him. " His mind is one of the finest reasoning engines with which I have ever come into contact, though, and it is not always easy to follow his trains of thought. I have a few ideas concerning the matter of which he has just spoken, but it would be presumptuous of me to attempt to explain them. It is perfectly possible that my conjectures are altogether mistaken in this matter."

At this moment, the maid Lucy entered to announce that dinner was ready.

" Shall we set an extra place for you, Doctor ? " Mrs. Alderton asked me.

" There is no need for that," I said. " Though it may seem a little melodramatic to say that I will keep watch, nonetheless that is what I will be doing in this room while you eat in the other. I will take my evening meal later. Please do not concern yourselves about me."

It was clear to me that the Aldertons were both frightened at the prospect of the shadowy doom that Holmes had foretold.

Sherlock Holmes never uttered such warnings lightly, and following the departure of the couple to take their meal, I therefore positioned myself by the window where I was able to keep watch on the comings and goings through the front gate of the garden. I had been watching for some thirty minutes, by my estimation, when I espied Holmes entering the gate. I made my way to the front door to let him enter.

" You have caused Mr. and Mrs. Alderton a great deal of worry, not to say fear, by your words," I told him.

" I have to confess that this was indeed my intention," he answered, with no hint of apology in his voice. " I have just returned from telegraphing Hopkins at the Yard," he informed me. " I have requested the presence of some local constables to stand guard here, and ensure that no ill befalls the Aldertons. After I had dispatched my message, I made my way to the police station where I had requested a reply be sent. I am happy to say that Hopkins immediately recognised the importance of my communication, and he himself will be arriving here later this evening. Ah, here are the promised reinforcements," he added, gesturing to two uniformed constables who were entering the driveway. " Excellent."

He moved to the front door to admit the two, who introduced themselves. " Your Inspector has no doubt informed you that you are to protect the couple currently occupying this house, who are presently eating their evening meal, and after they have removed to a place of safety, to stand watch and arrest any person attempting to enter."

" Yes, sir, that was made clear to us," affirmed the older policeman, a grizzled sergeant.

At that moment, the door to the drawing-room opened, and James Alderton entered. He appeared taken aback by the presence of the two police officers, but addressed himself to Holmes.

" You said earlier that we might have to leave the house. You are suggesting that we make arrangements for a stay of several nights ? "

" Indeed so, though I trust that your sojourn away from here will not be more than one of two or three days' duration. You may also tell the girl Lucy to do the same. For the moment, these upstanding officers are here for your protection. But believe me, there is danger to you and your wife only while you are in this house. Once you are elsewhere, you will be safe. It is the house, not you, which is the object of the rogues' attention."

" You relieve my mind a little," replied Alderton. " I will inform my wife of what you have just told me."

" Would they really be in danger if they stayed ? " I asked Holmes after Alderton had left the room.

" Indeed so. The ruffians I expect to confront will stop at nothing to achieve their ends."

" Mahoney and his accomplices ? "

" Not Mahoney," he answered me with a thin smile. " Mahoney is here in this house."

" What ? " I exclaimed, but Holmes was given no chance to answer me, as Inspector Hopkins, accompanied by half a dozen of his men, some of whom were carrying bulky sackcloth-wrapped bundles, made their way to the front door, and Holmes moved to admit them.

" Thank you, Mr. Holmes," Hopkins said to him. " As you suggested, I ordered a special train and came here immediately. The accommodation is already reserved by now, I trust, and Jessup here," indicating one of his men, " will escort the Aldertons there."

" And are you prepared for the evening's entertainment ? "

" We are armed and ready to meet what may come our way," Hopkins said stoutly.

" Very well. Then let us wait until the Aldertons are ready to depart. Then the fun will start."

It was at least thirty minutes before Alderton reappeared to inform us that he and his wife were ready, during which time Hopkins' men had dispersed themselves around the house, standing guard at the entrances. As Hopkins had informed us, one of the police officers summoned a four-wheeler, and the Aldertons took their places inside, while the maid sat with the driver. Mrs. Wiles, the cook, was seen off the premises by another policeman.

" Good," remarked Holmes. " We have at least secured their safety. I am convinced they know nothing."

" No more do I," I complained. " What is happening, and what did you mean when you told me that Mahoney is in this house ? We have not seen or heard anything that would lead us to that belief."

" There are other senses beyond those of hearing and sight," Holmes remarked to me.

I considered this. " I now comprehend you. How horrible to contemplate."

" We must act while there is still daylight," Holmes told Hopkins. " Your men have brought suitable tools with them, I perceive."

" Indeed so, just as you requested, Mr. Holmes."

" Let us test their suitability, then," replied Holmes, and led us to the conservatory.

The stench was as foul as I remembered, and Hopkins commented, " It is hard to believe that no-one recognised this," he remarked. " Very good, men. You may tie the cloths about your faces, and dig where Mr. Holmes directs."

" There, and there," Holmes told them, pointing to two spots some six feet apart on the conservatory floor. Dig gently, and extend the hole towards the other party."

A few minutes' excavation revealed a ghastly sight. A body, in a state of some decay, but with the face still just recognisable as that of Mahoney, was lying in a shallow cavity beneath the floor of the conservatory. It was possible to make out that the deceased had suffered a heavy blow to the head—so heavy, indeed, that the skull appeared to have been crushed at the point of impact. The constables turned away in disgust, as did Hopkins. Holmes stood his ground, but I could tell that the sight had affected him also. As for me, I should have been inured to such sights, having seen my share and more of battlefields, but my stomach heaved, and it was all I could do to keep myself from disgrace.

" I had not expected him to be in such a state," Holmes admitted. " One of you men, summon the mortuary van, and warn them what to expect." He extracted a handkerchief from his pocket and tied it about his face. " I do not expect this to repay any dividends," he said, " but it must be done." He bent to the loathsome corpse, and ran his hands through the tattered rags that draped its form. Eventually, he stood up and ripped the cloth from his face, revealing an expression of disgust. " I must wash," he said briefly, and disappeared in the direction of the kitchen.

" No point in standing here, men," Hopkins said to the police officers. " Go back to your places and keep watch." The men moved off, with expressions of relief. " Come, Doctor," he said to me. " Let us await Holmes in the drawing-room. I take it that we have just viewed the remains of Monsignor Mahoney ? "

" I would not give my oath in court about that without further examination, which I am reluctant to carry out," I answered him, " but I would lay a considerable sum of money on it. The general physique, what I could make out of the hair and what remained of the facial features, would all lead me to that conclusion."

" And who put him there ? And why ? "

" There we will have to wait for Sherlock Holmes' theories. I have none of my own."

At that moment, Holmes entered. His face was pale, and he was perspiring slightly. " Many pardons. I had hoped by now that I was accustomed to such sights, but it appears that there are still some that affect me. Watson, do you think that Alderton would object if we were to take a small amount of the spirits I see in the decanter there ? From the colour I would guess it to be an old brandy, and I feel we are all in need of a small restorative, are we not ? "

" We can easily make good any losses," I smiled, moving

to the decanter and pouring some of the drink into three glasses.

" Ah, thank you," Holmes said, accepting his drink. " I feel a little better now. These weaknesses may be nothing of which I should feel ashamed, maybe, but it is hard to see them in any other light. Well, as I prophesied some months ago, Mahoney put his life in jeopardy when he fled Ledbury Hall. I can only assume that his whiskey-drinking friends were the agents of his death, quite possibly in search of the letter, which, of course, they did not find."

" How do you know they did not find it ? "

" Because, my dear Hopkins, the supposed tramps and the applicants for the servants' post were all sent to look for this letter. The discovery of Mahoney's body has cleared up a number of mysteries."

" I can see that we now know his fate," said Hopkins. " What other problems have been laid to rest ? "

" We can be certain that those who were responsible for his death were those who dispatched the serving-girls to this house, in other words, those posing as Edwards & Lowe, the servant agency." Holmes related to Hopkins a brief account of our visit to the agency the previous day.

" They are seeking the letter that Mahoney took with him ? "

" I can see no other explanation."

At that moment, we heard the sounds of a scuffle, and raised voices from the area of the kitchen.

" Halloa ! " remarked Hopkins. " It would appear we have visitors."

" One visitor, I would say, judging by the sounds," Holmes corrected him. " Let us go and interview Mr. O'Reilly, or whatever the name of our visitor transpires to be."

❋

DON "JUAN ALVAREZ"

–

WINDSOR

E made our way to the kitchen, where two of the constables were restraining a struggling figure, who, at the sight of Holmes, ceased his attempts to work free of the restraining arms, and stood, his mouth agape.

" No Irishman here," said Holmes, looking at the form of Alvarez, whom we had previously seen in his capacity of butler at Ledbury Hall. " This is indeed a surprise, is it not ? "

" I had not expected to see you here, Mr. Holmes," said the Spaniard, in some confusion.

" I confess that your presence here is equally unexpected

to me," said Holmes. " I take it you are not searching for
Monsignor Mahoney ? "

" Indeed not. I assume you and these gentlemen have
discovered his body ? " He indicated the constables who
had relaxed their grip on him.

" What do you know of that ? " Hopkins asked him. " I
have half a mind to arrest you on suspicion of the murder
of—"

" Gently, now, Hopkins." Holmes laid a restraining
hand on the Scotland yard detective's sleeve. " I rather
fancy that Señor Alvarez is after the same quarry as are we,
and for the same reasons. I have very considerable doubts
as to whether he was responsible for the death of Monsignor Mahoney. However, I am still mystified as to how he
knew how to come here."

" How do you know this man ? " Hopkins asked.

" He is the butler at Ledbury Hall."

" Allow me to correct you, Mr. Holmes." Alvarez spoke
up. All trace of subservience had vanished from his voice,
and his tones were those of a proud Iberian nobleman addressing his equals. " I used to work as the butler at Ledbury Hall. I am, however, a man with my own private
means—you might well refer to me as a 'gentleman', and
I entered and left Lord Ledbury's employ of my own free
will, albeit at the request of the late Cardinal Tosca. The
name Alvarez is not the name I was born with, I need
hardly add, but I will not burden you with the full list of
my names and titles unless it becomes absolutely necessary
for me to do so."

" You knew Tosca before the unfortunate incidents at
Ledbury Hall, then ? "

" Indeed I did. I knew him well as a friend. Perhaps you were unaware that in the past he had served as

Archbishop of Toledo, my hometown ? "

" I believe that Mahoney informed us of that fact. That is where you became acquainted ? "

" More than simply becoming acquainted, we became and remained fast friends. Perhaps I may tell you of some of the background to all this ? "

Holmes glanced at Hopkins, who nodded his assent.

" May we sit comfortably in the drawing-room or some place other than here ? " asked Alvarez. " I have no intention of attempting escape, I assure you, Inspector, and I am sure my story will be of interest, even though it is a little lengthy."

" Very well," Hopkins answered him, and we thereupon made our way to the drawing-room, where Alvarez, now installed in an armchair, with a constable flanking him on either side, continued with his story.

" My family is of some consequence in the area, and we met socially on a number of occasions attended by others of our class. We shared a common interest in music, and a liking for the vintages of the area—though I never saw him drink to excess, you understand, he was a connoisseur of wine. One circumstance particularly attracted his attention—the fact that my mother was English, and I therefore was brought up to speak English and Castilian with equal fluency. We exchanged views on a variety of different subjects, and he was especially interested in the aristocracy of this country who had preserved the faith of their forebears, of which my mother was an example.

" He preserved the hope that this country would once again return to the fold of Rome and place itself under the care of the Holy Father. As you know, this seemed for a long time to be a fantasy only, with little basis in reality. But then Tosca, living in Rome, but with whom I maintained contact through letters, discovered that one of the British Royal family had an interest in returning Britain to Rome. Even though this might appear a remote possibility to some, Tosca believed that it was worthy of his attention, and proposed that he visit England at some time to explore the situation in some more detail.

" Naturally, if his visit were to take place, it would be necessary for it to be undertaken somewhat *sub rosa*, and to that end, he it would be necessary for him to stay at a private house, rather than involving the hierarchy here in the business. Ledbury Hall would be the obvious place chosen by the British government, given Lord Ledbury's connections with the Vatican, and Tosca proposed to me that I should undertake, on behalf of the Church, the somewhat unusual mission and adopt the strange, for me, temporary calling in which I first met you. The Cardinal felt that it would be useful for him to know the contents of the discussions between Lord Ledbury and the other members of the English establishment when he was not present. To that end, he could either suborn one of Lord Ledbury's servants, or he could introduce his own agent into the household and keep an eye on events through such an agent.

" The choice fell on me, for the reasons I have just described. However, I can tell you that the goals of His Eminence were not the same as mine. Though my sympathies are naturally with Mother Church, my experience of life and of men had taught me that such a move as Tosca was seeking to promote would result in something approaching disaster. His Eminence, though a good man, had lived a somewhat unworldly cloistered life by many standards, and I think that he failed to foresee some of the practical difficulties of his project. When he proposed this plan to me, my first instinct was to refuse, despite our friendship. When I came to consider the matter a little more closely, however, it seemed to me that I could save His Eminence from his own well-intentioned plans, which seemed to me to have little or no chance of the success he anticipated for them. Were he to fail, as I suspected would be the case, at his attempted scheme of reconciliation, his standing within the Vatican would be low. As it was, my aim was to be less than truthful when it came to reporting the conversations between Lord Ledbury and the English politicians. By presenting a somewhat more gloomy picture of the situation than was actually the case, I hoped to be somewhat of a brake on the process.

" As it turned out, it was relatively easy for me to achieve the goal of employment at Ledbury Hall. When I was younger, my parents had employed an English butler. It was relatively easy for me to imitate his mannerisms and so on, and to pass myself off as an experienced butler. It was easy for me to explain that I possessed some English as well as Spanish blood, which of course is nothing but the truth. I added that I had been working outside England, and His Eminence was kind enough to provide me with references stating that I had been previously in his employ.

" It was clear to me from the start that Lord Ledbury was a good man who saw it as his duty to serve both his country and his Church to the best of his ability, and I told the Cardinal as much in my letters to him. There was no doubt in my mind that he was the perfect host for the Cardinal when he came to visit, not only from the point of view of his extensive political connections, but also because of his equable temperament and his sound judgement.

" It was clear to me, even before the Cardinal's arrival, after I had listened to some of the discourse between the

English politicians when they considered their conversations to be private, that there would be little need for me to present a more pessimistic view of the situation than was actually the case. To a man, including Lord Ledbury, they were against the scheme, and only the fine English sense of fair play and courtesy allowed the Cardinal's visit to proceed.

" Let me add that there was no personal ill-will at all. Those involved had met Cardinal Tosca on a number of occasions previously, and all expressed their happiness at meeting him again, and their personal goodwill towards him.

" When the Cardinal arrived, though, I was filled with dismay. Though I knew that Monsignor Mahoney was attached to the Cardinal's household, I had not expected to see him in England on a mission of this delicacy."

" You knew Mahoney previously, then ? " Holmes interrupted.

" Yes, indeed. We had met on a number of occasions in Rome, and I can tell you quite frankly, though it may weigh against me in your eyes, that we were not on good terms. He struck me as being a hot-headed kind of man, who through his impulsive actions was quite likely to bring harm to himself and possibly to his master as well. I am sure that you are aware that he was associated with the Fenians—not only to the cause of freeing Ireland from British rule, but also to the cause of violence. I have proof that he was a member of one of the most radical groups in the movement."

" Proof, you say ? " demanded Hopkins. " Can you substantiate that allegation ? "

" Indeed I can. This paper may prove of some interest to you." The man we knew as Alvarez withdrew an envelope from his breast and passed it to the police officer.

" Most interesting," said Hopkins, after he had opened the envelope, and unfolded and perused the paper contained therein. " Should this paper here prove to be genuine, and the truth of its contents confirmed—"

" You may have no doubts concerning that," said Alvarez. " This list of names will prove to be completely accurate, rest assured."

" In that case, Her Majesty's Government owes you a considerable debt. These names are of great interest to those organs of the Government who are concerned with such matters. I may tell you almost without hesitation that should any charges be brought against you in connection with this matter, this would go a long way in mitigation."

" If that is an attempt to persuade me to confess my guilt in the business of the death of Mahoney, I hate to disappoint you, Inspector. I am totally innocent of any involvement in the matter."

" In that case, how were you aware of Mahoney's death ? " Hopkins demanded.

" Through my presence in a small office in Upper Holland Street, where Mahoney and his conspirators would meet. Naturally, they were unaware of my presence when I learned of his death. The office was known to me previously, as I had been following Mahoney's movements after my departure from Ledbury Hall."

" The office was taken in the name of Edwards & Lowe ? " Holmes suggested.

Alvarez bowed slightly. " Indeed. That is the name on the door, at any event. I perceive that your reputation is well-deserved, Mr. Holmes. This address in Holland Street was ideal for their purposes. The band had leased two adjoining rooms. These were arranged in such a way that there were two doors, located in a fashion that rendered it impossible to see one from the other, and leading to two separate exits from the building. This allowed members to arrive and depart by separate routes, confident that they would be unseen and unnoticed."

" I have been there," Holmes told him.

" Very good. Then you no doubt noticed the tall cupboard beside the door connecting the two rooms, which could be accessed from either side ? "

" I did."

" This was my hiding-place for several days last week. I entered the building in the morning with a small stock of provisions, and spent the day there, letting myself out when the coast was clear. I wished, first and foremost, to discover the whereabouts of Mahoney. Since he had fled Ledbury Hall, I was aware of his whereabouts in this house. For more than several weeks, though, he had not been living here, as the house had been taken by an English couple, and I had not seen him entering the building at Upper Holland Street. It was my belief that he was in possession of papers, which I had not seen, which would set this country at war with itself.

" Though I was frightened of being discovered, I determined to make my entrance at a time when the office was unoccupied, and to listen to any conversations that might take place in the office. To avoid any untoward discovery, I wedged the doors in such a way that it would take time to open them; sufficient time, I hoped, for me to be able to make my escape by means of the other door, should anyone try to force their way into my hiding-place. I heard the gang discussing the death of Mahoney, whom they had killed here in this very house. They had been frantic in their attempts to force him to tell them of the whereabouts of the letter which I am sure you are currently seeking. They are desperate men, and I can assure you that the methods they used to persuade him were brutal. He succumbed to their torments and died in agony, if their account is to be believed. What I heard made me even more afraid for myself should my hiding-place be revealed."

Despite myself, I shivered. " Does any man deserve a death such as that ? " I could not prevent myself from ejaculating.

" Most certainly not," the Spaniard agreed. " Though I had no love for Mahoney, I pray for his soul after such a terrible fate has befallen him. His killers were unable to find the letter they sought, as you are no doubt aware. Though they had emptied the house of all his effects, and had searched diligently, it had proved impossible to locate it. They were convinced, however, that it was here in this building, believing that Mahoney would never have abandoned it or let it out of his possession. It was their intention to enter the house tonight or tomorrow night, and remove Mahoney from his hiding place while renewing their search for the missing paper."

" You raise an interesting point there," said Holmes. " Why did they conceal the body of Mahoney in this way ? Why did they not dispose of it in another way ? The River Thames is not that far distant."

" As I understood from what I heard, a kind of superstitious horror came over these men as they came to a full realisation of what they had done. The idea of taking the body out of the house was repugnant to them, and they determined to conceal the body, empty the house of all personal effects, and come back later to dispose of the evidence.

" However, much to their surprise, the agent was un-commonly quick at re-letting the house, and they were un-able to gain access to the house which they had previously assumed would remain empty for some time. They dis-guised themselves as tramps at the start of the new lease, in an attempt to find their way inside, but their attempts were rebuffed. The so-called 'agency' of Edwards & Lowe then sent girls to seek non-existent positions. I have no doubt that these were the wives or the mistresses of the conspirators, who would be instructed to search for the missing document, and present it to them."

" And you, too, are in search of the missing letter, I may assume ? " said Holmes. " This is no doubt the reason for your being here ? "

The other smiled. " Quite the contrary, my dear sir," he said, reaching inside his coat, and drawing out another en-velope, which he handed to Holmes, who took it, opened it and examined the contents with a thunderstruck air.

" I think that you owe us an explanation of all of this, Señor," he said to the Spaniard.

" Very well. As I say in this message, which I was in-tending to leave for the Fenians who no doubt will be pay-ing a visit in the near future, the letter from your Royal Catholic is no longer in existence."

" What ? " both Hopkins and I exclaimed as one.

" Yes, indeed. When Lord Ledbury sent me upstairs to find the letter, as I described to you earlier, I swiftly invent-ed a reason why I should not give the letter to him imme-diately upon his return from London. In truth, since this was the evening of the Cardinal's death, I was overcome by emotion, and I found it impossible to think coherently.

" I spent the night with the fatal letter tucked under my pillow, hardly sleeping, though I was exhausted by the events of the evening and their consequences. In the morning, though, I knew what I had to do. Since the Cardinal was dead, the letter had little more use. I could not trust myself to give it to Lord Ledbury, as he is too honest a man to keep it hidden. He would have felt duty-bound to give it to a member of the British government, or even worse, return it to a representative of the Church. Either of these alternatives could be a cause of friction or worse, which I had no wish to see.

Equally distressing to me was the state in which the body of Tosca had been left. Your brother, Mr. Holmes, had given orders that the body was to be left untouched, and the room sealed until a detective—by which I may assume that he meant you—arrived to take charge. This was repugnant to me in the extreme. I mentioned that His Eminence was more than a name to me. He had been a good and trusted friend, and I was disturbed by the thought of his body sitting in its gore in the dining-room.

" Suddenly, it occurred to me that it was possible for me to kill two birds with one stone. I could dispose of the letter and respect my friend's memory at the same time. I knew that it would be useless for me to attempt to enter the room from the hallway, but the French windows could be forced from the garden with the aid of a flat-bladed knife.

" At midday, therefore, when all the other servants were eating their meal, I slipped outside, and made my way into the dining-room. With some difficulty, as he was a large man, I assisted my late friend to be comfortable and dignified in death. I did not remove the dagger, though."

" Why not ? " asked Sherlock Holmes, who had hardly moved a muscle during this remarkable narrative.

" Because it was I who had given it to him many years

before when he left Toledo. He had often expressed his admiration for the famous products of my hometown—the Toledo blades—and expressed his whimsical disappointment that as a prelate of the Church, he was not permitted to enjoy the ownership of one. I therefore had this made. Perhaps you noted the arms emblazoned on the hilt ? No ? I am disappointed there. If you had noted them, you would have seen that the arms to which Tosca was entitled as a prince of the Church were present."

" The heraldry of the Roman Catholic Church is one of the few subjects with which I am not intimately acquainted," remarked Holmes, drily.

" Well, be that as it may. In any event, I had an aversion to withdrawing the dagger from the corpse. Once my friend was arranged with some decency, and his eyes had been closed, I took the letter and secreted it under his clothes. I was confident that it would not be discovered for some time, if at all. As you know, when I entered the room to talk with you and saw that you had moved His Eminence, I was concerned lest you had discovered the letter at that time."

" But Lord Ledbury informed us that you had presented the letter to him, and he had put it in his safe, whence it later disappeared," I pointed out.

" That is very true. I presented Lord Ledbury with the envelope, which bore the Royal coat of arms on the outside, and into which I had previously inserted a sheet of thick paper. I trusted to his sense of gentlemanly conduct and fair play that he would never open the envelope."

" He might have passed it to the government or handed it back to the Church," objected Holmes.

" Indeed he might, but in that case, who would be at fault ? Not I, surely. As it turned out, this was no problem. Mahoney used the key that had been stolen on his behalf from the Whitehall office and abstracted the envelope."

Hopkins spoke for almost the first time during this narrative. " That must have been a shock to him," he chuckled.

" I am sure it was, and I confess to feeling some pride at having foiled his tricks in this way. The other papers on which my late friend and Mahoney had been working, by the way, I removed from the dining-room, and returned to the room which had been assigned for use as a sitting-room by His Eminence and Mahoney."

" That would explain why papers I would have regarded as being confidential were to be found on the table in that room, when I would have expected them to be locked away in the boxes. These were all the papers that you took from the dining-room, other than the one you hid on the Cardinal's body ? " The other nodded. " Were you aware, by the way," added Holmes, " of the existence of a document, signed and sealed by His Holiness, ready for the signature and seal of the British Royal personage ? "

The Spaniard's eyes went wide with horror. " No, on my life ! His Eminence never said anything about this to me. I had no idea that matters had progressed to that stage."

" Neither, apparently, had any other person," said my friend. " Since the paper was found at the bottom of the box, it is likely that Monsignor Mahoney was also unaware of its existence."

" Where is that document now ? "

" I am not at liberty to disclose its precise whereabouts, but I can assure you that it is now in a place where it can do no damage," replied Holmes.

" Be that as it may," interrupted Hopkins. " All of this is most interesting, and I may well believe that you are not responsible for the death of Mahoney, but I would like to know exactly why you are here this evening."

" I think I can explain a little of that," said Sherlock Holmes. " The paper that I have been handed is addressed to whom it may concern. It explains that the letter that the addressees—presumably the Fenians—are seeking is no longer to be found in this country."

" I can explain this. Following His Eminence's death, you will recall that his body was removed to the local undertaker's while it was decided what further steps should be taken, and where he was to be interred. Many messages on this subject passed between London and Rome, I believe, while His Eminence lay unburied. I lit candles and prayed for his soul, but it was a source of considerable concern to me that he had not received Christian burial and the rites of Mother Church."

" The body was preserved, I take it ? "

" Indeed it was. It was decided that it would be refrigerated, rather than embalmed. Only a month ago, it was decided that the body would be returned to Rome for interment in the crypt of one of the churches there. Accordingly, it was transported from England, and I received word this morning that the funeral rites were conducted two days ago. We can be sure that the letter was buried with him, since I placed it inside his garments in such a way that it would not be discovered."

" I understand that the letter has now been laid to rest, but what I fail to understand is your reason for coming here and delivering this extraordinary message to the gang of Fenians."

" From what I overheard in my hiding-place, it appeared

to me that the gang would make their move on this house either tonight or tomorrow night. They planned to overcome their superstitious dread, and to remove Mahoney's body and search it. Should the current tenants interfere, they were to be killed."

" Are these men armed, then ? " asked Hopkins.

" Indeed they are. Not only do they possess weapons, but it seems to me that they are prepared to use them."

On hearing this, Hopkins gave orders in a low voice to one of the constables flanking Alvarez, who left the room. " I have just told my men to be prepared for this," Hopkins explained to us.

" In any case, I made my way here, and determined to wait for a suitable opportunity. If the present tenants were at home, I was going to explain that they were in danger, and persuade them to accept this letter to present to the gang on their appearance. My hope was that the contents of this letter would persuade them to abandon their scheme.

" As I was approaching the house, I noticed the tenants and a girl who is presumably their servant being escorted into a carriage by a man who was almost unquestionably a police officer. I therefore concluded that the official forces had, by some means unknown to me, arrived at a similar conclusion to myself. I was therefore expecting to be apprehended by your men, sir," to Hopkins, " when I made my way into the house."

" Well, you have certainly been a busy man," chuckled Hopkins, " but I think you were playing an overly dangerous game. You would have done much better to come to us, or even to Mr. Holmes here, with your suspicions and your knowledge."

" Maybe that is true," the other shrugged. " However, I

was not sure—indeed, I am still unsure—of my position as regards the law here."

" If the information you have provided to me here," Hopkins said to him, tapping the sheet of paper he had been given earlier, " allows us to capture these rebellious Irishmen, you have nothing to fear in that regard."

" And the actors appear on cue," said Holmes, a curious half-smile on his lips. " Hark ! "

We listened carefully, and could hear a noise at the rear of the house. Hopkins whispered to the remaining constable, who swiftly and silently left us. " Come," Hopkins said to us, almost inaudibly. " Are you armed ? "

I shook my head, as did Alvarez, but Holmes silently withdrew his favourite riding-crop from within his coat.

We started from the room to the conservatory, and were halfway there when a series of confused shouts broke out.

" Come, there is not a moment to waste ! " called out Hopkins, fairly bounding down the passage towards the source of the noise and blowing his whistle with all his might. We followed him, and a scene of chaos met our eyes. Three of the constables who had arrived with Hopkins were outnumbered by their opponents, with whom they were struggling. The unmoving bodies of several of the constables' comrades lay on the floor. Hopkins and Holmes sprang forward as one, Hopkins brandishing a heavy life-preserver, and Holmes his riding-crop, which they used to strike the constables' assailants, who soon went down under their blows.

Alvarez and I were not far behind them, you may be sure, and I used my experience of Rugby football to tackle and bring low one of the other intruders who had escaped the blows of our leaders. Alvarez, for his part, was gamely attempting to overcome another of the Fenians, who was wrestling him to the ground until I stepped in and laid the fellow out with a straight right to the chin.

As Holmes and Hopkins moved among the fallen cursing Irishmen, pinioning their hands with the handcuffs that Hopkins and his men had brought with them, I bent to provide succour to the fallen policemen. I was relieved to see that other than a few bruises and grazes, they were essentially unharmed. I offered what aid I could while Hopkins dispatched one of his constables to summon transport for the prisoners.

The growling captives were soon lined up against the wall, and one of them noticed the shallow grave from which Mahoney's body had been taken. " Where is he ? " he asked in a surly tone. " Is the letter with him ? "

" Ah, so you came for the letter, did you ? " smiled Holmes. " I have just had word that the paper you are seeking is far away from here, if indeed it still exists, in a place that will never be disturbed. You may seek it if you wish, but I fear that you will be doomed to failure."

" And who are you ? " asked the Irishman, with a foul oath.

" My name is Sherlock Holmes," answered my friend.

The effect on the other was electric. He staggered visibly, and turned to the others with a look of hopelessness written on his face before turning back to us. " It was you hiding in the cupboard, then, listening to us ? We found the bottle in the cupboard and none of us drinks that Spanish vino, so we knew we had visitors. If we had known that we were up against you, we might never have started this game."

Alvarez seemed ready to speak, but Holmes moved in front of him swiftly, smiling almost sweetly at the Fenian. " You may believe that if you wish," he answered. The

Irishman seemed ready to retort, but at that moment, the constable who had been sent for the vehicle entered, followed by several more policemen.

" Take them away," Hopkins commanded his men, and the prisoners were led away. " We have them in the bag, thanks to you, sir," bowing slightly to Alvarez, " and naturally to you as well," to Holmes. " And your assistance has been invaluable, too," he said, turning to me.

Mr. Sherlock Holmes

–

Baker-street, London

  t has been almost a complete failure on my part, from beginning to end." These were the words that Sherlock Holmes addressed to me a few days after the last, as we were sitting by the fire at our rooms in Baker-street.

" My dear fellow," I expostulated, " I really do not see how you can lay that charge at your own door in that way. A dangerous gang of Fenians is no longer at large, the murderer of Cardinal Tosca is no more, and the English public is happily unaware of the fate that potentially threatened it. Added to which, you have the personal thanks of His Holiness, expressed through Mycroft, and the spirit of brotherly love is once more abroad in the Holmes family."

Holmes smiled thinly. " The last is at least true," he admitted. " The telegram from Rome was as unexpected as it was welcome, and you are correct regarding the relations between myself and Mycroft. Such a state of affairs is welcome, of course.

" But the fact remains that I was culpably and negligently slow in so many aspects of the original case. I have to say that were it not for your observation of the dead man's fingers, it would have taken me considerably longer to determine the true cause of death."

" Ah, yes," I answered, with all the modesty I could muster. " I am most gratified to have been of assistance there. Have you determined, at least to your own satisfaction, exactly why Mahoney killed his master Tosca ? "

Holmes shot me a sharp glance. " Watson, I continue to underestimate you and your talents of perception. You have pinpointed the exact point at which I consider myself to have failed. I can consider several good reasons why the murder may have taken place. The most likely is that the Cardinal's notorious temper became too much for his secretary to bear. Even a Catholic priest is only human, and Mahoney was obviously a man with a fair proportion of self-love and pride in his makeup.

" Next, we may consider the possibility that Tosca had become aware of Mahoney's involvement with the Fenians, and was threatening him with exposure if he were to continue the association. It is not without the bounds of possibility that Mahoney determined to silence this threat to his career.

" And finally, there is ambition. Despite Mahoney's somewhat unprepossessing appearance and demeanour,

Mycroft received word from the Vatican that he was highly regarded in a number of somewhat influential circles there, and was destined, according to some, to rise in the hierarchy. From what we have heard, though, it would seem that Tosca would use his influence to block such an appointment."

" And then we have the sudden, unpremeditated type of murder," I added. " The type for which no satisfactory solution can be found."

" Alas, that will not work in this case," my friend answered me. " Remember the electric bell that killed Tosca. Premeditation of the most unpleasant kind. The use of the Toledo blade was, I believe, an attempt to incriminate Alvarez. Mahoney undoubtedly recognised him and saw him as an adversary."

" Have you determined Alvarez' true identity ? "

Holmes laughed. " My dear fellow. As soon as he had declared himself to be other than Alvarez, I recognised him. Even before that time I had marked him as a man who had not spent his life as a servant, and I was reasonably certain of his true name and rank. The way he moved was that of one used to command, rather than one used to being commanded, and the state of his hands indicated that manual labour was a practice to which he had only recently come." Here Holmes gave a name, but for the sake of discretion, I prefer not to repeat it here. The man whom we knew as Alvarez has recently come to occupy a senior position in his government, and it might cause not a little embarrassment were his previous activities to be revealed. I have sometimes wondered, though, what were Lord Ledbury's feelings on beholding the face of his former butler in the newspaper, as a minister in the Spanish

Cabinet.*

" But how did you make the connection between Mahoney and the Aldertons ? "

" You should be familiar with my discovery that a typewriter is as distinctive a means of communication as is handwriting. I remarked it previously in the case of Mr. James Windibank and his stepdaughter, Miss Sutherland, as you will probably recall. In any event, though the majority of the documents that we saw left behind at Ledbury Hall were handwritten by the clerks of the Holy See, there were some copies of letters that had been typewritten in England, one assumes by Mahoney, and had been produced using carbon paper.

" Though a carbon impression is less susceptible to analysis than one impressed directly by the typewriter ribbon, there were some points of interest that caught my eye at the time. The slight damage to the upper loop of the g, for example, coupled with the depression of the capital T relative to the rest of the line, and the slight nick out of the dot of the small I were sufficient to make a unique identification of this machine.

" As one does in these cases, I filed the information away mentally, not expecting to use it again once the case had been given up, but imagine my surprise when we encountered the same typewriter again in Upper Holland Street. I proved to my own satisfaction that it was the

---

*   Editor's note: Despite my best efforts, it has proved impossible to locate with certainty any member of the Spanish Cabinet of the year of 1914 who was possessed of an English mother. It is possible that Watson's notorious memory has failed him yet again as to the year of "Alvarez"'s government service.

same machine by typing a few letters of my own using it, and the recollection of the documents we had seen at Ledbury came to mind. It is amazing, is it not, how the mind can instantly summon into prominence, almost without effort, those facts that were learned previously but previously were discarded as seemingly being of little value ?

" This typewriter, of course, is also that used to type the name and address given to the girls and to write the letter to the letting agent ending the lease. We may also be certain that the note informing Mrs. Wiles, the cook, that her services would no longer be required, was written on the same machine. It is clear that following Mahoney's murder, the criminals wished to end the lease and dismiss the cook, but they felt unsure of their ability to imitate Mahoney's handwriting with sufficient skill to deceive the recipients of these documents.

" The typewritten nature of the cancelled lease, together with discrepancies between the signatures, and the dismissal of the cook were sufficient to tell me that Mahoney's departure had not been a voluntary one. It was also clear, after one smell of the foul odour proceeding from the floor, that Mahoney was still with us, though in a decomposed form.

" Given Mahoney's Fenian connections, and the Irish accent of the tramps who came to call at Windsor, I had no doubt that these were Mahoney's confederates seeking him. I had also deduced that the girls calling on the Aldertons and seeking employment were likewise attempts to gain access to the house, either to discover the paper themselves and hand it over to the gang, or allowing the gang members to effect an entrance for that purpose.

" The information supplied to us by Alvarez regarding the letter took me by surprise, I freely admit. I can offer no defence for my ignorance in that regard."

" And what of the Aldertons ? May I ask where they stayed the night ? "

Sherlock Holmes permitted himself what can only be described as a mischievous grin—an expression that I had hardly ever previously seen on his face, and one which I saw but twice subsequently. " Why," he chuckled. " Where would you guess would be the safest, best-guarded location in the fair town of Windsor ? "

" The Castle," I answered, after a moment's thought.

" And that is exactly where the Aldertons and their girl stayed for two nights, while their house was disinfected and made safe from any infection that the late Mr. Mahoney may have left behind, and any damage caused by his removal from the premises was repaired. Her Majesty was not in residence at the time, but the State Guest Suite was made available to them. I trust that Mrs. Alderton can adapt herself once more to the relative squalor of The Willows," he laughed.

" And the Royal personage whose indiscretions have caused so much trouble ? "

Holmes became serious. " I have heard from Mycroft that senior Ministers, not to mention the Archbishop of Canterbury, have been holding conversations with him, and that he has agreed not to make his conversion to Roman Catholicism public. He has further agreed that when the time comes for his coronation, it will be conducted according to the English, not the Roman rite."

" That is indeed a relief," I told him. " I believe that you may well have saved England from the horrors of a civil war."

" Not I alone, Watson," he said. " As I say, I regard most of my work in this case as having been a failure, and

I was, at the end, only one of many who helped to preserve the peace of the Realm. And I must now attend to the dreadful business at Upminster, the solution of which I expect to find in today's agony column". Having said this, he took up the day's *Times* and proceeded to scan it with interest.

Appendix

–

ACD's note

Editor's note: This letter, in the distinctive handwriting of Sir Arthur Conan Doyle, was enclosed with the sheets in which this adventure was set forth. The date at the top of the letter does not include the year, but for reasons I have given earlier, I believe it to be 1914, at which time the Duke of York as mentioned in this story would have become the reigning monarch, George V.

September 25

My Dear Watson,

I must thank you for the manuscript of the " Adventure of the Cardinal" that you sent me last week. At this moment in our nation's history, I feel it would be extremely inadvisable to release the facts contained therein to the public. I am sure on further reflection you will agree with me on this, and will come to the same conclusion as have I—that is, that the balance of the public's mind will be disturbed by the revelation of these facts. I therefore have concluded that this adventure should not be forwarded for publication.

However, notwithstanding my opinion on this matter, I found your account to be of immense interest, and further confirms my high opinion of Mr. Holmes as one of the greatest Englishmen who has ever lived, in every sense of those words.

I do, however, look forward to reading the account of the incident to which you alluded in your letter; namely, the capture of the German spy, and the way in which our mutual friend deceived the German High Command for so long. How I wish that I had been there with you to enjoy the look on Von Bork's face when " Altamont" revealed the truth.

Please pass my very best regards to Mr. Holmes, should you chance to encounter him in the near future, and naturally, the same good wishes extend to you. I look forward to renewing our acquaintance when you are next in the neighbourhood.

Yours sincerely

[signature]

Arthur Conan Doyle

OTHER BOOKS FROM INKNBEANS PRESS

THE DEED BOX OF JOHN H. WATSON MD: HUGH ASHTON

ONG thought lost, the box containing the untold tales of the great detective Sherlock Holmes, deposited in the vaults of Cox & Co. of Charing Cross so long ago, has recently come to light.

It was presented to Hugh Ashton of Kamakura, Japan, the maiden name of whose grandmother was Watson. Ashton has transcribed and edited the adventures he discovered in there, and they have been published by Inknbeans Press.

Eleven adventures from the Deed Box series, 360 6"x9" pages reproduced in the style of the original canonical adventures, and bound together for the first time as a hardcover volume.

These adventures of Sherlock Holmes are approved by The Conan Doyle Estate Ltd.

More at http://221BeanBakerStreet.info

THE BRASS MONKEY:
SUSAN WELLS BENNETT

DIGITAL BOXED SET of all four of the Brass Monkey novels: *Wild Life*, *Charmed Life*, *Night Life* and *New Life*.

Sun City, Arizona: where old people go to die.

he At least that's what Milo, a retired border patrolman, thinks when first arrives in the palm- and orange-tree-lined retirement community. He takes up photography to wile away his remaining days.

Before long, he is fighting and flirting with Claire, a young widow who is working through her trauma while volunteering at the zoo. He meets Sax, a former cop and the bartender at the Brass Monkey, and Sax's favorite barfly, Sondra.

Unable to turn off their suspicious natures, Milo and Sax see danger and intrigue simmering just beneath the serene picture-postcard settings of Arizona. And life will never be the same for any of them!

THE NICK WEST TRILOGY:
JIM BURKETT

COLLECTION of excitement, terror, heroes, villains, betrayal, revenge, government duplicity, madmen, chemical weapons, old scores, new vengeance, and lies exposed all under one cover.

Former DHS agent Nick West uses his skills with reasoning, and weaponry to stop an international cartel from selling United States to the highest bidder in *Declaration of Surrender*, a madman from selling a weapon of mass destruction so cruel and so indiscriminate even the governments vying to purchase it have second thoughts in *American Sanction*, and a killer out to avenge the death of someone who didn't deserve to die, and doesn't care who gets killed in the process in *Reprisal*.

INKNBEANS PRESS

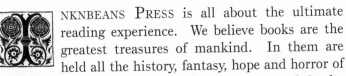 NKNBEANS PRESS is all about the ultimate reading experience. We believe books are the greatest treasures of mankind. In them are held all the history, fantasy, hope and horror of humanity. We can experience the past, dream of the future, understand how everything works from an atomic clock to the human heart. We can explore our souls, fight epic battles, swoon in love. We can fly, we can run, we can cross mighty oceans and endless universes. We can invite ancient cultures into our living room, and walk on the moon. And if we can do it with a decent cup of coffee beside us...well, what more can we ask, right?

Visit the Web site at www.inknbeans.com

Fresh Books Brewed Daily

Made in the USA
Lexington, KY
28 December 2013